FLIGHT TG-101 to NOWHERE

notionpress.com

FLIGHT TG-101 to NOWHERE

Subroto Sinha

notionpress.com

Notion Press

Old No. 38, New No. 6

McNichols Road, Chetpet

Chennai - 600 031

First Published by Notion Press 2016

ISBN 978-93-5206-826-5

Dedication

To my parents

Chapter 1

CIA Headquarters, Langley, Virginia

2 February 2013

The Director of CIA, John Epstein, was having an important meeting with the Director of Intelligence, Richard Crawley and the Director of National Clandestine Service, Harold Stacey in the bug-proof, well-guarded conference room. John was upset at the reports from his operators in Europe, about Russia developing a secret program of hacking the computer data networks of NATO and the Pentagon, with the help of Chinese computer engineers. He code named it "DRAGON."

He asked Richard Crawley, "Can you update me with the latest developments in this project? If they succeed in this program it will have a disastrous effect on the security of our data networks."

Richard sat grim-faced to his right, with a briefcase containing important files and compact discs. He quickly glanced towards Harold across the table before replying, "The situation is indeed very serious and demands immediate clandestine action. A top Chinese computer engineer, Aiguo by name, is the brain behind this program. In collaboration with Russian engineers, he has managed to break the supposedly impregnable passwords of some of the data networks. The program is able to keep track of the changes in the passwords, which make the frequent security password changes ineffective. The cryptographic techniques, which was considered to be very secure and hack-proof, is now in danger of being exposed. A software has been designed which follows the scrambling-unscrambling codes and retrieves the original data."

John, who had been listening with rapt attention, now commented, "It is a serious matter and must be stopped at all cost. How far are they from actually implementing the programs?"

"They are still in the experimental stage and trying to perfect a method of delivering the software into the target networks, without being detected," he replied and added, "If they succeed in their project, then even our military satellites will be under their control, as they would send the appropriate encrypted commands and retrieve the data."

John was a worried man and looked towards Harold Stacey and said, "Harold, this is your baby now! You have got to work at lightning speed to stop this project. You know we are the target and if they succeed then our entire country will come to a standstill. All our commercial, military and administrative functions will cease."

John dispersed the meeting, but not before announcing that he would meet every week on Wednesday to take stock of the situation.

Richard and Harold came out of the conference room and briskly walked towards their respective departments. As they neared the elevator, Harold turned towards Richard and said in a contemptuous tone, "It has always been like this; you guys deposit the shit and I have to do the scavenger's job. Why could you not ensure that this project never took off?"

Richard looked slyly at him, "These days the engineers working on clandestine projects have become very clever.

They work in their own countries, ostensibly on some innocuous projects and when they discover something important in the special project, they communicate with their international counterpart through cryptic messages in the internet. If they have to discuss something important, they go to a third country on the pretext of attending a seminar. Nobody suspects anything and the job is done!"

"Then how was this project discovered in the first place?"

"You could say it was by accident! Two years ago, one of our operators in Belgium intercepted a cryptic message mailed to an IP address in Syria. He decoded it and found it had something to do with the development of a computer program for retrieving information from encrypted data. He immediately alerted the operators dealing with computer crimes. They kept a close watch on the messages received and sent from that address. It was revealed that the messages came from an address in Russia and were redirected from Syria to an address in China."

Harold could not reconcile himself to the fact that a secret project of this magnitude could remain elusive from the hawk eyes of the CIA operators for such a long time. Noting the skeptic look on his face, Richard invited him to his room with a promise to show him some interesting reports.

Della Noel, the extremely attractive secretary of Richard, greeted them with a flashy smile as they entered the room. She had been managing the office of the Director of Intelligence, with the utmost efficiency, during the past five years. Besides being attractive, she was endowed with extraordinary intelligence and language skills, which made her an indispensible asset in the office. She was well conversant with seven languages, including Russian and Chinese. She accompanied Richard on a few important missions around the globe, where her skills were very useful.

"Any messages, Della?" Richard enquired, as he walked towards his chair, behind a huge oak table. Della briskly walked into an adjacent room and came out with a file, which she placed before him. He studied its contents intently and appeared satisfied. He closed the file and requested her to bring the file XX/Prog/03 on the current case.

She promptly brought the requested file, before disappearing into her room. He flipped across a few pages and stopped at a particular page. "Ah! There you are. This is the IP address of the computer located in the city of Lanzhou in North-Western China, where the messages used to be sent. This city is the center of transportation and telecommunication in north-west China. Here, in a telecommunication research center, worked a scientist named Aiguo, who was the recipient of the messages." Richard took the file to the conference table in the room and showed it to Harold, who was already seated on a chair in anticipation of the promised information. He took a close look at the information and also a photograph of Aiguo. He asked Richard if he could provide him more information about this man.

Richard extricated a floppy disc from the file and loaded it into the overhead projector. He held the remote control and projected the photo of a middle-aged man with spectacles and slightly bald, on the screen. He was standing at the entrance to a building, carrying a laptop on his shoulder.

"That is the Telecommunication Research Center and, apparently, he is working on a minor telecommunication problem," informed Richard. He moved to the next photo, where Aiguo is seen in the company of younger Chinese men and two women, in the tea room in his department.

"These are his assistants, of whom three men and one woman are also involved in the special 'hacking' project," he added.

"The next photo shows Aiguo with his wife, Chunhua, and a small two-year old daughter in the sitting room of their modest apartment. Chunhua is a computer expert and is a professor of Computer Science in Lanzhou University. She is also involved in the special 'hacking' project."

"This is a very important photo," said Richard as he projected the next photo. "This is Dr. Obukhov along with his beautiful assistant, Yelena Petrovsky. They live in the small town of Novgorod, to the north of Moscow. Dr. Obukhov is apparently a teacher of computer science in a local school, where Yelena is also a teacher. He is the principal Russian scientist working in the 'hacking' project."

"This photo gives the link between Dr. Obukhov and Aiguo," said Richard as he projected the next photo. "We can see Dr. Obukhov in an intense discussion with Aiguo during the tea interval at a conference held in Paris in March 2012."

"What more do we know about Dr. Obukhov?" enquired Harold.

"Not much, except that he is a divorcee and visits the department of mathematics, Moscow University, on weekends, frequently. He is generally accompanied by Yelena on these visits."

"What do we know about Dr. Obukhov's first wife?"

"The only information we have about her is that she is a medical doctor, by profession and now resides in Minsk.

There has not been any contact between the two during the last three years."

Richard closed the projector and returned to the file before him. After browsing through a few messages, he looked up at Harold and said, "Now you know why it was not possible to nip the project in the bud! The participants are scattered over different countries and they have left no trail of their participation. The only way we knew about the existence of this project is through the interception of the encrypted messages exchanged between the principal participants. In one message intercepted recently, the result of a trial experiment was vaguely discussed. We just got a hint that the trial was not very successful."

Just then, Della entered the room and whispered something to Richard. He got up abruptly and told Harold, "Sorry! I must leave now. I'll be in touch with you if I receive something important." He left the room hurriedly, prompting Harold to do likewise.

Chapter 2

ANDREWS AIR FORCE BASE, WASHINGTON D.C.

9 February 2013

Colonel Herman Turner, an ace fighter pilot of the US Air force, had been earlier posted in the island of Diego Garcia, the US military base in the Indian Ocean. He had flown many sorties successfully during the Iraq war and in Afghanistan, to flush out the Al-Qaida terrorists who had taken refuge in that country. He was a test pilot whose job was to find the suitability of the aircrafts which are being purchased by the US Air Force. He was now posted to the 89th. Airlift wing of the air force based in Washington D.C. This unit is responsible for worldwide special air mission airlift, logistics and communications support for the President, Vice President and other U. S. senior leaders. The responsibility of Air Force One, the Presidential plane, is assigned to this wing. He had also worked closely with the CIA in air dropping operators in hostile territory, or air lifting them to safety when they were in danger of being detected. Harold Stacey of CIA was given the important mission of ensuring the abortion of the joint software project between Russia and China, at any cost. He conjectured an important role for this island in the mission and thought it appropriate to discuss the finer details with Herman.

***

Diego Garcia is a tropical coral atoll located south of the equator in the central Indian Ocean. It is approximately

3650 Kms. east of the coast of Africa and 1790 Kms. south south-west of the southern tip of India. It lays in the Chagos Archipelago at the southernmost tip of the Chagos –Laccadiva Ridge – a vast submarine range in the Indian Ocean. It was part of the British Indian Ocean Territory till 1966. The original inhabitants were the plantation workers, known as Chagos Islanders, or Chagossians. They were mostly slaves brought to the island from Madagascar and Malay.

The Americans were interested in having a base in the Indian-ocean area, so that they could be nearer to the regions of conflict in the middle-east and Afghanistan. The British allowed them to use Diego Garcia as a military base, in exchange for cancelling a $14 million British debt for military hardware purchase. It was ideal for a military base due to its seclusion and sparse population. The Chagossian settlers were forcibly sent to Mauritius and the Seychelles and the island was made off limits to reporters, the Red Cross and all international observers. The only inhabitants of the island, now, were the military personnel and civil support staff who were building the base facilities.

The island was soon developed into a modern base with runways for the landing/takeoff of large planes and berthing facilities for warships and aircraft carriers. The Military Sealift Command (MSC) of the US Navy that controls most of the replenishment and military transport ships of the Navy became solely responsible for the department of Defense's ocean transport needs, in 1970. It projected the three basic requirements of the Navy as sea shield, sea strike and sea basing. The key element in sea basing is afloat prepositioning in certain ocean areas. Prepositioned ships remain at sea, ready to deploy at short notice the vital equipment, fuel and supplies to initially support US Army, Navy, Air Force and Marine Corps in the event of a contingency. During the Iraqi invasion of Kuwait in August 1990 three ships of Compsron 2 (Acronym for 'Commander Maritime Prepositioning Ship Squadron 2') sortied, delivering a Marine Expeditionary Brigade (MEB) to Saudi Arabia for participation in the Gulf war. The MEB is a formation of the Unites States Marine Corps, a Marine Air-Ground task force of 14500 Marines and Sailors, a reinforced infantry regiment and a composite Marine aircraft group. Other COMPSRON2 ships offloaded the munitions, bombs and fuel on Diego Garcia that were required for the American bomber fleet. As a result, the B-52Gbombers flew more than 200, 17-hour bombing missions over 44 days and dropped more than 800,000 tons of bombs on Iraqi forces in Iraq and Kuwait. In October 2001, USA commenced military operations from Diego Garcia using B-1, B-2 and B-52 bombers to attack enemy targets in Afghanistan, after the 9/11 bombings in New York.

In addition, Diego Garcia base is one of only a handful of locations equipped with a Ground-based electro-optical deep space surveillance system for tracking objects in deep space. It is part of the United States Space Surveillance Network that has the capability of monitoring the earth's surface, including moving objects.

***

Harold Stacey was aware of the military potential of Diego Garcia and added to it, is its complete isolation. It could be used effectively for any clandestine operation, without anyone else in the world knowing about it. He called at Herman's office and was escorted to his room. After the usual greetings, he asked Herman, "Are the runways long enough for the safe landing of a commercial airliner, like the Boeing 777?"

Herman thought for a while before answering, "Well! In the case of an emergency landing, it is possible. In fact, this airport is designated as ETOPS (Extended range Twin engine Operations) emergency landing site for all large commercial airliners. In the case of regular operations, the pilot has to be well trained to land on a short runway and lift- off from the same."

"That's good! I am not going to land here in a commercial airliner, but, may be, a large commercial airliner may land here soon!" quipped Harold.

"Hey! What are you up to? Is it another covert operation bringing prisoners to that place?" asked Herman sarcastically.

"No! Not at all! You know our Government is very sensitive to human rights violation. We will not do anything that may even suggest we're indulging in this heinous crime," replied Harold with a twinkle.

"Whoa! Watch who's telling! I've lived in that island long enough to know what goes on behind the curtain of secrecy. Now, come out with the truth!" insisted Herman.

"Since you insist, I must tell you that there will be a covert operation soon and you will be solely responsible for doing it," informed Harold.

"No! Not me! I have been doing these things for a long time and I'm tired of it. I want to rest now in a cushy job in Washington D.C. You have to find somebody else," said Herman forcefully.

"I wish I could! You're the best in this line and in such operations, only the best is given responsibility. You know, a failure would be disastrous for the country, including us. It is a very delicate job and has to be done with the utmost finesse and intelligence. Director CIA has entrusted this mission to me, under authority from the President and it has to be done as early as possible. Your services will be transferred to us until this mission is completed," revealed Harold.

"You've given me no chance and you know that, as a patriot, I cannot refuse a responsibility given to me from the highest authority," lamented Herman. However, you must give me the complete outline of the operation, so that I can work out all the details, meticulously."

Harold agreed to confide the details of the operation to him after two days, at the CIA headquarters. He told him to be ready to fly to an unknown destination at short notice.

Chapter 3

CIA Headquarters, Virginia

14 February 2013

John Epstein called another emergency meeting to take decisions on the serious crisis looming ahead in the aftermath of the discovery of "dragon." Richard Crawley and Harold Stacey were present, as usual. They represented the two important action centers in any National crisis. Richard began by explaining the latest information on the "dragon." Our sources in Russia informed us that Dr. Obukhov and his assistant, Yelena, are planning to visit Thailand ostensibly on a vacation, during the period, March 13 to 19. They have booked a flight in Aeroflot airlines.

John remarked, "It's strange that they are going on a vacation at this time, to Bangkok of all places. The schools in Russia are not closed. It appears a little odd."

"Your suspicions are justified," admitted Richard. "Our undercover agents in China have informed us that Aiguo and his wife, Chunhua, have not been seen in Lanzhou since March 1. Enquiries revealed that they have both gone to Thailand to deliver expert lectures in a workshop, which is organized in King Mongkut's Institute of Technology, Bangkok. They are scheduled to leave Bangkok on March 19 and visit London to participate in a conference."

"There you are! Both the collaborators have cleverly arranged a meeting in Bangkok. I'm sure the other Chinese collaborators working with Aiguo are also attending the workshop," commented John.

"Yes, indeed! They are also attending the workshop. There is another important news that we received. The Chinese and the Russian team members are booked in the same flight to London" remarked Richard.

John looked towards Harold and asked, "Have you formulated any plans on 'dragon'?"

Harold got up to project a flight route map from the projector. He said, "Our information is that they are all flying by the non-stop flight TG-101 of Trans Global Airlines to London. It is a Boieng 777-200 aircraft with a capacity of 440 passengers. Its flight path is over Myanmar, Bangladesh, Nepal, Kazakhstan, Russia, Belarus, Poland, Germany and Netherlands, as shown in this map. Our plan is to capture alive all the passengers in this plane, including those working in the project 'dragon."

"How are you going to capture alive so many passengers?" interrupted John. "The intention to keep them alive is good, so that we come to know what research they have already done. We can then make use of them to work for us. But, what will be the use of the other passengers who are not associated with this project?"

"We cannot release them, because, if we do that, the whole world will come to know the truth behind the capture. Thc entire operation has to be kept a closely guarded secret," said Richard emphatically.

John nodded his head in agreement and added, "I still feel that capturing so many people will be a very risky operation and I'm not sure if it is within our capabilities. How will you capture them?"

"It is very much within our capabilities," replied Richard. "We simply ensure that the plane does not land in London, but instead, lands in our air-naval base in the Indian Ocean, Diego Garcia. It will be immediately taken to the underground hangar and kept till our work is over."

John stared in disbelief at the simplicity of the operation, as presented by Richard. He finally exclaimed. "Richard, you are perhaps aware that there is a surveillance network with numerous radars and satellites in space that are tracking the aircraft to ensure that it is following the prescribed flight path. How are you going to evade detection while diverting the flight path?"

"Simple again!" replied Harold. "We fly low to avoid detection by radar and blank the arriving signals from the surveillance network instruments. While diverting the flight path we shall use DRFM[1] jamming, which deceives the radar into believing a false position and altitude of the aircraft."

"Fine!" remarked John. "What about ACARS[2]automatically sending various flight and engine information to the ground stations. The position of the aircraft will be known to the ATC[3] and ground staff and if they see an aircraft suspiciously changing its flight path without any apparent reason, they will be alerted. Can this device be switched off from inside the aircraft, by the pilot?"

Richard intervened to say, "It's difficult, as the pilot has to go through a trap door in the gallery behind the pilot's cabin and enter the passage containing rows of circuit breakers. He has to pull out the right circuit breaker connecting the ACARS. Only an experienced pilot can do it."

Harold agreed and added, "The time when the aircraft crosses Thai radar airspace and enters Myanmar air space, is the right time to turn off the transponder[4] and disable the

ACARS. There will be no 'squawk'[5] and the aircraft would be completely off the radar grid. This is the time to turn the direction of the aircraft, without being detected."

John was still skeptical about the assertion that the aircraft cannot be detected. He turned towards Harold and asked, "What about the satellite pings[6]sent periodically to the SATCOM[7] aboard the aircraft? From an analysis of the time between the ping and the response it is possible to work out the distance of the aircraft, which is a circumference of certain radius from the satellite."

Harold was quick to answer, "The ACARS transmission is disabled by disabling the VHF and SATCOM channels. So, although the system is not completely switched off, it cannot transmit to the receiving stations."

John felt partially relieved to hear that avoiding detection is not an unsolvable problem. But, now another thought seized his attention, "How will you prevent any passenger from using his mobile, which will give away the position of the aircraft?"

"No passenger will be in a position to use his mobile. The aircraft will ascend to an altitude of 45,000 feet, when the pilot will use manual pressurization to depressurize the aircraft's pressure to the air pressure outside. This will cause the oxygen masks to deploy, providing passengers oxygen for 12 to 20 minutes. After that, hypoxia would set in and passengers would lose consciousness. The pilots are provided oxygen for a longer time. By that time the aircraft would be flying over the Indian Ocean at a low altitude," answered Harold confidently.

John appeared impressed and requested Harold to project the whole plan of operation as it would be executed.

Harold projected the magnified map of the Indian Ocean containing the surrounding countries of South-East Asia, the Indian subcontinent, the islands of the Bay of Bengal and the Indian Ocean island of Diego Garcia.

"Trans Global Airlines Flight 101 leaves Bangkok at 0.30 hours local time. It crosses the Thai- Myanmar border at 1.45 hours. The transponders are switched off and the ACARS disabled. The aircraft turns southwestwards to the Bay of Bengal Sea. It climbs up to an altitude of 45,000 feet and manually depressurizes. After flying for 30 minutes in the same altitude, it descends to an altitude of 5000 feet, during the next 30 minutes. By now it is somewhere over the middle of the Bay of Bengal in this area as shown by the pointer. About 4 hours would have elapsed by now. The destination coordinates will be set to the coordinates of Diego Garcia and the aircraft will fly over international waters, straight to its destination. It will land in Diego Garcia, about 5 hours later and will be taken to the underground hangar. All these operations will take place during the moonless night hours. The next part of the operation will be conducted by Richard's men."

1. *Digital Radio Frequency Memory is a repeater technique that manipulates received radar energy and retransmits it to change the return the radar sees. This technique can change the range the radar detects by changing the delay in transmission of pulses, the velocity the radar detects by changing the Doppler shift of the transmitted signal, or the angle to the plane by using AM techniques to transmit into the side lobes of the radar. By analyzing received signal strength from side and back lobes and thus getting radar antennae radiation pattern, false target can be*

created to directions other than the one where the jammer is coming from.

2. *Aircraft Communications Addressing and Reporting System. It is an automated communication system used by commercial aircrafts to transmit and receive messages from ground facilities, like, airline maintenance department, aircraft or system manufacturer, etc. It relies on VHF (Very high frequencies)*
3. *Air Traffic Control*
4. *Transponder is a combination of transmitter and responder. It is a device of identifying aircrafts to the ground controller*
5. *ATC units use the term 'squawk' when they assign an aircraft a transponder code, e. g., 'squawks 7654.' It means select transponder code 7654. When the aircraft flies into the jurisdiction of another ATC beyond the current radar airspace, the code has to be reassigned. If the transponder is shut off the aircraft remains unidentified.*
6. *Ping refers to a utility used to test the reachability of a host on an IP network. The ping is sent once every hour to all the receiving peers those respond to it signaling their network presence. It is used as probes to check the availability of SATCOM systems aboard the aircraft.*
7. *SATCOM is a radio system that uses a constellation of satellites used to transmit voice, data, or both. ACARS can make use of SATCOM to transmit its data to ground stations.*

Richard took a deep breath before beginning to reveal his part of the operation.

"The plan of the operation so far enunciated has been meticulously planned. Every possibility has been considered and extensively debated before finalization. The chance of a failure is very low, but one cannot rule out some unexpected glitches. A team of doctors will examine the condition of each passenger as they are evacuated and taken to a waiting hall. The passengers who are in our 'wanted' list will be separated from the others and taken to another hall. The next day they will all be put in a B-52 bomber and flown to Edwards's air force base, Nevada, with service halts in the American bases in Qatar and Lajes Field, Portugal. From there they would be taken to the Test and Training Range in Area 51, where they would be interrogated."

"In the meanwhile, the TGA aircraft stationed in the hangar would be dismantled and all the avionics, including the black box, would be deactivated. The parts will be loaded into a C5 – Galaxy plane and flown to the southern Indian Ocean, where it will be dumped over the deepest part of the ocean, so that there would be no record about the existence of the aircraft. Of course, our government would actively participate with the other nations, in searching the missing aircraft and condemn those responsible for committing this crime. They will have no knowledge about the operation 'dragon.'"

At this stage John interrupted, "Undoubtedly, your project has been meticulously planned, but who are the people chosen to execute this project? Success or failure depends upon them."

"They are the best in the business! The execution team will be headed by Colonel Herman Turner, whose impeccable record of service with us and the U. S. Air Force cannot be matched by anyone. He will be assisted by three men chosen by him. I have already requisitioned their services using the powers vested by the President. My assistant, Della, whose knowledge of the languages will be an asset, is also in the team"

"Oh, Herman! I know him very well. We have worked together during the Iraqi operation. His knowledge is amazing!" remarked John.

John looked pleased at the way operation 'dragon' was progressing. He ended the meeting after announcing that he would be in close touch with his lieutenants during the course of the operation.

Chapter 4

18 February 2013

Colonel Herman Turner flew to Diego Garcia in a Stealth Fighter jet to make necessary arrangements for operation 'dragon.' He had chosen Lieutenant Sid Mathews working at Andrews air base, as one of his partners in this mission to accompany him. He made a quick survey of the number of planes and military personnel in the island. He visited the underground hangar and saw seven fighter jets stationed inside, undergoing routine maintenance checks. He figured that only two jets can be accommodated if the Boeing 777 is to be brought inside the hangar. The other planes must be sent to other bases on some pretexts. The lone aircraft carrier stationed near the island has to be sent to the Persian Gulf area on a routine exercise, to keep it away from the coming activities on the island.

Herman chose three more partners from this island base to work in the mission. They were Major Paul Scott, an expert in avionics who had flown all kinds of planes during his decade and a half service with the air force, Lieutenant Will Tucson and Lieutenant Alan Murphy, who were ace pilots and participated in the Afghan arena. He asked them to keep only two planes and fly the rest to the bases in Iraq and Turkey, along with some of the personnel. Only a skeleton staff should remain in the island during the period 19 to 22 March. He cautioned them to ensure that the evacuation does not arouse their suspicion.

Herman, along with Sid, flew to Paris air base in the stealth fighter. Here he was met by Della. She was looking more attractive than ever before, in her tight-fitting, double breached, high waist, black skirt and white, flowery chiffon tops. Although Herman had seen her before in the course of his meetings with Richard, he had never seen her new, elegant hair-do and facial make-up that elevated her to the pedestal of a Greek goddess. He flashed a smile and a gentle bow, which was reciprocated by her. They proceeded towards the base commander's office.

They were seated on a sofa when an operator of the CIA came and handed them a sealed envelope. "These are your new passports and new identities." Looking at Herman, he said, "You are a businessman named, Peter Morris, an expert in electronics, having a small semiconductor factory in Westmont, Illionis. Della is your wife, Margeret, with an interest in Oriental arts. You are both visiting Thailand as a tourist. You will board the Trans Global Airlines, Flight TG-115, from Heathrow airport, London at 14.30 hours on March 15 to Bangkok. You will leave on 19 March by flight TG-101 of Trans Global Airlines, along with the Chinese and Russian scientists. You are booked at the Shangri-La Hotel in Bangkok, where those scientists are also staying. You are not to carry any of the old identities with you. Your mobiles and laptops have been replaced by new ones. Even your suits, clothes and other recognizable items have been replaced. You have to memorize your new identities before you leave. Any other questions?"

Herman looked puzzled and said, "I guess that is the rule of the game and I have to abide by it. But, is there any address or phone number in Bangkok which I can reach in case I have some problems?"

The operator took out another envelope from his briefcase and handed it to him, "This is the name, address and phone number of our operator in Bangkok. He will contact you as soon as you arrive in your hotel. He will keep you updated on all information concerning this mission. "He departed after wishing them "Good Luck."

Herman and Della were transported by a NATO helicopter to the army base near London. From there they were taken to the Grand hotel in central London. They were booked in a family room, as they were supposed to be husband and wife.

They went up to their eighth floor room, accompanied by security personnel, who searched the room thoroughly before handing over the door key card. Herman relaxed on the sofa after locking the door securely and Della stared out of the window to enjoy the view of London.

"Sorry, Della! I have to be your husband for a patriotic cause. But, don't you worry, you can divorce me anytime!" chuckled Herman, looking at Della.

"I've done such patriotic duties many times, but, woe be to the husband who attempts to take liberties by crossing the line. You know, I'm well versed in karate, with a black belt rating. So, no husband should do anything silly to provoke me!" warned Della with a smile.

"Oh, no, never! I'm not that silly! I love myself very much and would like to remain in one piece as long as I can," remarked Herman. "I am wondering if this fear of the black belt has got anything to do with eligible bachelors being reluctant to propose to you!"

"Now come on! There is no dearth of proposals. It's I who decide which proposal to encourage and which to reject outright!" snapped Della.

Just then a call came on Herman's mobile. It was from John Epstein wishing him all the best for his daring mission.

"This is my last contact with you until the successful completion of 'dragon.' From now onwards you are on your own. God forbid, if anything unpleasant happens to you, we disown any connection with you. If you succeed, nobody will applaud you."

"I'm fully aware of it, Sir!" replied Herman before disconnecting.

He took out a cigarette, lighted it and sat in a thoughtful mood releasing smoke rings into the air.

"How strange life is! If a soldier in the battlefield kills a couple of enemy soldiers and gets killed in the process, he is hailed a hero and decorated with medals posthumously. Here I get killed incognito while fighting a very powerful enemy who is trying to destroy our country and I am shunted to oblivion and disowned by my own countrymen!" he talked loudly to himself.

Della heard him and said, "You should not worry about what others say, or think. A name only identifies the physical body, but not your soul, which carries your deeds to eternity. You are just carrying out the deeds that the Creator has ordained."

"It's a good consolation to think that way. Now, tell me honestly Della, do you not feel that your life is being wasted in such dangerous missions, when you could lead a very nice, secure life elsewhere?"

"No! I'm happy doing all this for the country. I don't think I'll be happy in a secure life elsewhere."

Herman looked at his watch and found it is time for dinner. He and Della got dressed for dinner and went down to the dining hall. They were joined by Lieutenant Sid Mathews who had also come down.

"Tomorrow we shall be flying by the same kind of aircraft in which we are returning with our guests. This will be the final opportunity for a rehearsal of our plan of action. You will select a seat in the first row while taking your boarding pass," said Herman in a businesslike manner, looking at Sid.

Della was busy browsing the menu card for ordering, when Major Scott also joined them. After greeting Della and Herman he said triumphantly, "I am an acute diabetic patient, so please consider it before ordering."

Everyone laughed! Major Scott was also given a fake identity. He was Mr. Ken McNamara, an Irish gentleman residing in London. He is suffering from acute diabetes and needs to inject insulin every four hours. According to British airport security laws, an acute diabetic patient is allowed to carry insulin bottles, along with syringe and needle, in his handbag, provided he has a valid doctor's certificate. He is visiting Bangkok to participate in his son's wedding anniversary. His son and daughter-in-law are residing in Bangkok.

They all had a hearty dinner, ending with drinks, before bidding each other good-night and retiring to their rooms.

Chapter 5

The afternoon of 15 March 2013, saw Herman and Della, as Mr. Peter Morris and his wife Margaret, seated in the middle row of the Boeing 777 Flight TG-115 to Bangkok. They occupied the two seats next to the aisle in the left hand side of the plane. Major Scott, as Ken McNamara, occupied the aisle seat, two rows behind them. There were no words exchanged between them and they pretended not to know each other. Sid occupied a seat in the first row. He observed the crew members as they walked up and down the aisle serving the passengers. Herman and Della behaved like a young couple on a holiday. A Chinese couple sat in the row behind them and Della could not restrain herself from talking with them in their native Chinese. They were overwhelmed with joy at hearing an American speak their local language. They told her that they were residents of Bangkok and had visited London on a holiday. They volunteered to guide Herman and Della during their stay in Bangkok.

The plane landed at the busy Suvarnibhumi airport, Bangkok, after a ten hour long flight. It was lunch time on the local clock. Della was confused with the time and date, as they were moving east and gaining in clock time. They collected their baggage and proceeded towards the exit. They saw a man standing with a placard having the name "Mr. and Mrs. Morris." At first they tended to ignore it, but soon realized that this was their identity during their stay in Bangkok. Herman nodded to the man and placed their luggage at his disposal. He led them to a plush car and opened the rear door inviting them to be seated. He put their luggage in the boot behind and proceeded to the driver's seat. Herman turned his head around to notice Major Scott entering the following car.

An hour's drive through the busy roads of Bangkok took them to the Shangri-La Hotel, on the banks of the river 'Chao Phraya.' The bellboy took their luggage to the allotted room on the fifth floor, overlooking the river. Herman noticed that Major Scott was given the adjacent room. He looked at the lunch menu and ordered steak, with French fries and salad, for himself and Della, to be delivered in his room. They entered the washroom in turns, to freshen up after a long and tedious flight. They were in deep slumber after lunch, when the intercom began ringing. Herman looked at his watch and found it was six in the evening. The desk operator was on the other end informing him that Mr. Kaseem Kaya was waiting for them in the lounge. Herman recollected that this was the name of the CIA operator stationed here, which was given to him in London.

Herman and Della dressed up quickly before leaving for the lounge. On the way Della reminded him that henceforth they would address each other by their fake identities only. As they entered the lounge they were greeted by a stocky, middle-aged man with a bald pate and circular-rimmed spectacles. He introduced himself as Kaseem and said he was asked to look after all their requirements during the stay. Peter (alias Herman) and Margaret (alias Della) extended their hands to acknowledge his greetings.

"I hope you are comfortable in this hotel, Mr. Morris," he asked.

"Of course, we are! I wanted to discuss with you about our requirements," said Peter.

"Yes, I know, I know! My man would meet you tomorrow morning in your room to deliver certain articles. Meanwhile, you can see the tourist spots of Bangkok during the four days that you are here," he said.

"I'll be glad to see those spots," said Margaret. "Can you arrange a cab to take us there?"

"Yes, indeed! I've made all the arrangements. Would you like to have some drinks, Mr. and Mrs. Morris?" he asked

"A glass of gin for me," said Peter. "A lemonade for me, please," said Margaret.

He motioned a waiter and asked him to bring the drinks. He leaned forward and said in a low whisper, "Your friends, the Russian and Chinese scientists are in the fourth floor of this hotel. They usually come down for dinner in the dining room at nine p.m. You can meet them there, but, you must be careful. They are constantly being watched by the KGB and other security agents in disguise. The slightest suspicion on their part might spell doom for you."

Kaseem took leave and promised to send his man in the morning with certain articles and information regarding cab for sight-seeing. Peter and Margaret bid him goodnight and retired to their room.

Breakfast was served in the room at eight in the morning. Peter and Margaret got dressed and then Peter called Ken McNamara (alias Major Scott) on the intercom and asked him to come over to his room for breakfast. Ken came over with his breakfast tray and made him comfortable in one of the chairs around the dining table.

"How was your first night in Bangkok?" Peter enquired.

"Splendid!" answered Ken, "but awfully quiet, considering the boisterous nature of the Thai people."

Margaret, dressed in a pink skater summer dress, was busy serving tea for everyone from their respective pots.

The intercom rang and Peter picked it up. The desk operator informed that a gentleman wishes to speak to him.

"I am Chaiyo and sent by Kaseem to give you some articles," echoed the voice.

"Come up, we're waiting," replied Peter.

Soon the door buzzer came to life and in walked a skinny young man in his thirties, carrying a handbag. Peter motioned him to be seated in the sofa.

After greeting everyone, he took out three cardboard boxes containing 9mm Browning Hi Power semi-automatic pistols and said, "Kaseem told you to always keep these pistols with you for self-defense, when necessary. I will take them back when I drop you at the airport."

He then took out what looked like a ball point pen. He handed it to Peter and said, "This is actually an instrument for generating a powerful laser beam that can be used in breaking open the electronic lock on the pilot's cabin door. I'll show how it can be used."

He took out a box with a lid that can be locked by using a remote controlled electronic locking system. He locked the box and demonstrated it by trying to forcefully open the lid. He then took the laser pen and directed it towards the lid and pressed a button that generated a thin pencil of laser beam. The lock opened immediately. He surveyed the amazement writ on everyone's faces and grinned.

"It's a very powerful tool which is mistaken as a ballpoint pen. It can also be used to focus the laser beam on the eyes of an attacker, to blind him temporarily," he added.

Peter felt satisfied and confident that he was well equipped for carrying out the initial part of the operation. Ken was getting impatient to see if his ampoules of insulin found any use in the scheme of things. “What about those ampoules of insulin and the syringe? Any use for it!” he asked.

“Yes, of course! It is the most important part of the operation. You have to first clear the way to the door of the pilot’s cabin, before the start of the other operations.”

He took out one ampoule from his bag and kept it on the table.

“This ampoule contains a liquid which looks like insulin, but it is not insulin. If a small dose is injected into someone’s body, he will become unconscious within a few seconds and will remain in that state for around four to five hours. You need to pump the liquid into the syringe very carefully,” he said, before handing over the box containing the ampoules to Kim. “You must now replace the box of insulin with the box of this ampoule,” he added.

“What about our sight-seeing tours, as promised by Kaseem?” asked Margaret in desperation.

“Yes, I have not forgotten it, madam. I have brought my tourist taxi to take you round the city. We can start immediately, if you’re ready.”

Kim said he would take a few minutes to get ready and join the others downstairs.

Peter changed over to a three-quarter length jean trouser and tee-shirt, taking into account the hot weather. Margaret wore the same summer dress and they both ambled towards the waiting taxi. Kim joined them few minutes later. They all wore straw hats and dark glasses to protect themselves from the summer heat of the sun.

Chapter 6

Bangkok 17 March 2013

Chaiyo's taxi was an SUV from the General Motors stables. It was well maintained and seemed to be used sparingly for special purposes. He opened the rear door and invited the trio to be seated. He closed the door softly after they were seated and rushed to the driver's seat.

"What would you like to see first? Thailand is home to a multitude of artists, painters and sculptors and the Bangkok Art Galleria is the place where critically acclaimed, contemporary art can be seen from the collections of several galleries all under one roof," asked Chaiyo.

Margaret jumped at the idea of art and expressed her desire to start the tour with this place.

Peter remarked, "You are a lover of Oriental arts and so this is the right choice to begin our tour." Ken supported him and added, "I was also once upon a time an artist of sorts until I joined the Air Force, where all my artistic tastes got buried."

"The clusters of art galleries are located in the Jewelry Trade Centre on Silom road. The galleries are: Thavibu Gallery, which has the best Thai, Vietnamese and Burmese modern art; Tang contemporary art, which has both Chinese and Thai paintings, sculptures and installations; and lastly Number 1 Gallery, which has exclusively Thai modern art from some of the most promising artists," informed Chaiyo.

Margaret's face lighted up on hearing the name, 'Jewelry Trade Center.'

"South-east Asia is known for its precious and semi-precious stones, especially the colored gems, such as sapphires, emeralds, and rubies," she remarked.

"You're right, madam. This place had been the home of gems and precious metals in Thailand for over 15 years, with stones from Sri Lanka, Myanmar and Thailand. It is the best place to buy without any worries."

They reached Thavibu Art Gallery and Chaiyo, acting as the tour guide, began explaining, "Thavibu takes the name from the three countries it represents; Thailand, Vietnam and Burma (Myanmar). It has a collection of more than 1000 paintings which are amongst the best available. Some of the paintings are sold to International buyers at a very high price and some are sold in the prestigious auction houses, like Sotheby, Christie, etc."

Peter nudged Margaret and said, "May be, you should purchase some valuable paintings for your art collection from here."

Margaret smiled and replied, "I think you're right! Why don't you present me a painting of my choice like a good, loving husband!"

"Sure! I'll be honored if you permit me to present you a painting. Go ahead and make your choice."

They went through the gallery admiring the paintings and the one that moved Ken the most, was a Vietnamese painting depicting a scene during the American occupation of Vietnam. He could not help remarking, "When two giants fight, it's the poor ants that get trampled!"

Chaiyo guided them to the next gallery, the Tang Contemporary Art. "This was founded in 2000 to present mainland Chinese contemporary art to an international audience," he said. "Currently, the gallery promotes critically acclaimed paintings, sculptures and installations from Chinese and Thai artists."

After spending about half an hour, they moved over to the final gallery, the Number 1 Gallery.

"This gallery shows the best of Thailand's modern artists and deals with mostly native Thai collectors and art lovers," said Chaiyo. "It reflects the gradual change of Thailand into a fully industrialized state, with the pressures of modern life."

After spending some time in this gallery, Peter felt it's time to have lunch somewhere.

"Why don't you have a typical Thai meal," suggested Chaiyo. "The ideal Thai meal is a harmonious blend of the spicy, the sweet and sour and is meant to be equally satisfying to eye, nose and palate. It may include soup, a steamed dish like mussels in curry sauce, fish with ginger, a hot salad (beef slices on a bed of lettuce, onions, chillies, mint and lemon juice) and followed by sweet desserts, or fruits such as jackfruit, papaya, grapes or melon."

"Well then! Take us to a restaurant for a typical Thai meal," requested Peter, while the others nodded in agreement.

After a sumptuous Thai meal they got ready to proceed with the next stage of their tour.

"Our next place of visit will be the Rattanakoshi Exhibition Hall, located on RatchdamneonKlang Avenue. Here you will get to experience the history of Bangkok through a series of film, music and computer displays. One of the most interesting displays explores the life in a palace and the royal customs. There is also a circular room which brings the different trade streets to life and literally makes you walk through Bangkok life. On the fourth floor there is a famous coffee shop, from where you can enjoy panoramic view of LohaPrasart temple and the Golden Mount temple," announced Chaiyo.

Peter, Margaret and Ken had a two hour tour of the exhibition hall, after which they decided to have coffee in the famed fourth floor coffee shop.

"It's good that we saw the city of Bangkok in this exhibition hall. I don't know if we shall get another opportunity to visit this city," remarked Peter, over a cup of coffee.

"It's amazing to see how this city, which began as a small trading center on the bank of the Chao Phraya River 200 years ago, has developed into a modern city, but the glory and grandeur of its past still prevails. The customs, the habits and the temples of the past still remain," observed Margaret.

Ken nodded in agreement and added, "The people are peace-loving and follow the teachings of Buddha, unlike us, who poke their nose in every country's affairs and often get a bloody nose in the process!"

"We are the patriarch of the world and the other countries are like our children. We have to admonish them when they misbehave, or help them when they are threatened. This is the responsibility given us by the Creator and we have to abide by His diktat," said Peter sarcastically.

"Where are we going next? Probably that will be the last stop of the day?" asked Margaret.

"We shall be visiting the biggest wholesale and retail flower market in Bangkok, the Pak KlongTalad. It has all kinds of popular flowers and flora-related items, like roses, forget-me-nots, orchids, lilies and many other exotic flowers and sold at very cheap rates in packs of 50 or 100 flowers. It is located on ChakPhet road near to the old city," said Chaiyo.

They arrived at the market and were amazed to see the variety and quantity of flowers present.

"Aha! Allow me the liberty of presenting you a bunch of roses, as your beloved husband," said Peter with a bow, looking towards Margaret.

"Yeah! That is the cheapest gift you can give to your beloved wife. I was expecting a diamond necklace, or a beautiful painting as a gift!" Replied Margaret mischievously. "Perhaps, I overestimated your financial status before the proposal!"

Peter grinned and said, "I suppose the cheapest gift would be a kiss. It costs nothing!"

"Oh! No, not in the marketplace!" replied Margaret with a blush.

Ken was enjoying the friendly exchanges. He looked at his watch and said, "Perhaps, it's time to go back to our hotel and prepare for our dinner encounter."

Chaiyodropped them at the hotel and promised to come in the morning at nine.

Peter and Margaret walked to their room followed by Ken, a little later. They rested for a while and then got ready to go down for dinner at nine. Ken told them that he would keep a watch on them from a distance.

Margaret was dressed in an attractive evening gown and Peter wore a new dinner suit. As they entered the dining hall they saw a group of Chinese men and a few women clustered around two tables joined together. A little distance away, around the corner table, sat a Chinese couple, and a Russian couple. Margaret figured they were Aiguo with his wife Chunhua, Dr. Obukhov and Yelena Petrovsky. Peter and Margaret sat around an adjacent table.

Margaret observed that Aiguo was reading a Chinese newspaper as Chunhua and Yelena were engaged in conversation. Dr. Obukhov was scribbling something in a notebook. Margaret took out a compact powder case from her purse and gently flipped it over the edge of the table to make it look like an accident. The case rolled over towards Aiguo's table. She got up promptly from the chair to fetch it. Aiguo also bent over to pick it up.

"Sorry, it slipped out of my purse," she said apologetically in Chinese.

"No matter! It's OK! You speak Chinese very well," he said with a smile.

Chunhua took over the conversation and asked, "What made you learn Chinese. It's a difficult language and Europeans don't usually like it?"

"I am a lover of Oriental painting and was interested in learning the Ming dynasty paintings. So I joined the Zhejiang School of painting for a year. I learnt Chinese before I joined and then brushed it up during my stay," replied Margaret confidently in Chinese.

The Chinese couple appeared impressed with her Chinese conversation and were beginning to open up.

"We are computer engineers and have come here to deliver lectures in a workshop organized at the King Mongkut's Institute of Technology. What is the purpose of your visit?" asked Chunhua.

"We have come on a holiday. My husband owns a small semiconductor factory in USA and I teach art in a local school. These days the computer is used extensively in works of art. I wanted to study graphics, but could not do it so far," replied Margaret.

"Oh! That is my special subject. Come to my place in Lanzhou and I'll make you an expert in graphics in two months," said Chunhua.

Margaret smiled and thanked her for the invitation and said she would consider it seriously.

Yelena now asked in Chinese, "Did you visit the art galleries here?"

"Yes, we visited all the galleries today. They were very impressive. I could have spent several days studying them," replied Margaret.

Dr. Obukhov asked in broken English, "Do you know Russian?"

"No! Not at all. I'd love to learn it though," Margaret lied.

Margaret heard Yelena speak to Dr. Obukhov in Russian, "Isn't she very pretty? I'll keep her husband busy and you can spend more time with her, teaching her Russian!"

Dr. Obukhov asked Margaret, "Your husband seems to be very quiet. He doesn't like to join our conversation."

"He doesn't know either Chinese or Russian. It's good in a way, otherwise he would not have allowed us to talk!"Margaret replied.

They all had a good laugh. Peter understood that they were enjoying at his cost and so he decided to display his sporting spirit by joining in the laughter.

Dr. Obukhov now moved over to sit next to Peter. He extended his hand and said, "I am Dr. Obukhov. What shall I call you?"

"I am Peter, not 'Peter the Great' the famous Czar of Russia!" he said, which exuded loud laughter from Dr. Obukhov.

Yelena was heard asking Dr. Obukhov in Russian, "Why don't you share your jokes with us, so that we can also join in the laughter?"

Dr. Obukhov translated Yelena's question and requested Peter to join them. "We all understand English fairly well and you can converse with us."

Peter requested the waiter to join the two tables, so that they can sit together. They ordered dinner, took photos of each other in their I-phones and ended by having drinks. As they left the dining hall they wished each other "good-night" and promised to have dinner again the following night.

Peter walked towards his room, along with Margaret, but as he approached the door he found it was unlocked. He asked Margaret to wait outside with her pistol ready and carefully stepped in with his pistol cocked up and put on the lights. He inspected every nook and corner of the room, the washroom and the wardrobe, but could not find anything suspicious, He saw a bundle of the laundry on one of the dining chairs and concluded that the housekeeper might have forgotten to lock the door after his exit. He called Margaret in and said that everything was clear.

Margaret was still not convinced that the room was free of bugs placed in inconspicuous places to eavesdrop any conversation. Her years with the CIA made her aware of the tactics employed by the KGB agents to listen to a suspect's conversations. She took out an instrument that looked like a CD player, which can detect any bug in the room. She operated it for a few minutes, but the result was negative. Reassured that their room was safe, they changed into their sleeping dress and went to sleep.

Chapter 7

Next morning Peter and Margaret got up early and dressed up before ordering breakfast. They waited for Chaiyo to show up and take them for the tour on the last day of their stay in Bangkok. Instead, Kaseem came to their room at nine to give them some important information. Their seats in Flight TG 101 have been booked. They have only to collect their boarding passes at the counter. He showed them the seat numbers, along with a diagram of the seating arrangements in a Boeing 777 aircraft. He also showed the seat numbers of the other members of the team. Sid Mathews was given a seat in the second row close to PeterKen had a seat two rows behind. Will Tucson and Alan Murphy were given aisle seats a couple of rows behind. This arrangement was made to make Sid, Peter and Margaret visible to them.

Kaseem divulged another important information, "It appeared that there was an attempt to track your new identities through the websites of the usual search engines. It is not known who the tracker was and which country he belonged to. But, it can be guessed that it must be the KGB."

At this point Margaret interrupted and said, "It is the practice in the CIA to substitute the appropriate bio-data in the websites, which are in conformity with the new identities whenever they are given. It is deleted as soon as the need is over. So, a search from any quarter will not reveal the true identities."

Kaseem nodded and said, "Yes, I know, I know! I said this only to caution you that you have succeeded in arousing the curiosity of the enemy. You have to be watchful."

Peter related the incident of the open door the previous night which gave him a fright.

Kaseem remarked, "Your room has been properly 'sanitized' by our men and one of the housekeepers, who is our man has been told to keep a watch on the room. He checks it daily and has probably forgotten to lock the door. You need not worry."

He then advised them to go downstairs where the tourist van is waiting. "Today is your last day in Bangkok. Your Flight is in early morning at 2 a.m. The taxi will come to pick you at midnight and drop you at the airport. My man will accompany you. You can give the pistols and ammunitions to him. Go to bed early so that you are fresh for your job."

Kaseem left the room, followed by Margaret and Peter. On the way they stopped briefly in front of Ken's room to inform him about the booking of their seats and also to give the message to the other boys in the team. Ken expressed his inability to accompany them, as he had a headache.

Chaiyo was waiting in the van. He greeted them with a smile and said, "Today, I shall take you to see the temples. There are about 500, but I shall take you to a few big ones only. Then we shall go to see the "floating markets," where dozens of wooden row boats float on the water, each laden to the brim with farm-fresh fruits, vegetables or flowers. If time permits, I shall take you to the riverside of Chao Phraya River to see the beauty of the Bangkok skyline."

Margaret was excited to see the temples, but Peter appeared quiet and serious. "Are you not well, today?" she inquired.

"I'm OK!" he said. "It's just that I'm not in a mood today. Can we return early? I have to settle many things."

"We can drop the market and return after the temples," she suggested.

Peter and Margaret had a quick lunch on the way after seeing the temples and requested Chaiyo to drop them to the hotel.

They walked briskly to their room and Peter carefully opened the door, to check if there are any signs of an intruder. He locked the door from inside after they had entered. Margaret brought out her instrument, as usual, to check the presence of any eavesdropping electronic devices. They both sat down to relax on the sofa and also mentally perform the operations to be carried out, once again.

There was a ring in the intercom and Peter took the call. Kim was on the line requesting an audience. Peter asked him to come right away and opened the door lock. Kim told him that he had passed on the information to all the boys, advising them not to contact each other and behave like strangers. "They are in high spirits, eager to do the job," he added.

"Have you given a syringe with the ampoule to Sid?" Peter asked.

"Yes, I have kept four disposable syringes, along with ampoules in my handbag," he replied.

Just then, another ring came in the intercom making everyone in the room alert. Peter walked hesitatingly to take the call. A strange unknown voice was heard on the line. It took some time for Peter to identify it.

"Is it Peter Morris?" the voice inquired.

When assured it is, the voice said, "Good evening, Peter! I am Dr. Obukhov. How was your trip today?" he asked.

"Oh, splendid!" replied Peter. "We came back a little early, as I was having a slight headache."

"How is it now?" he asked.

"I took a cup of hot coffee, a little siesta and the pain has gone," replied Peter.

"Good! The purpose of my calling you is that we are not coming for dinner tonight, as we have been invited for dinner by a Professor in the Institute where we are teaching. It is a farewell dinner as we are leaving tomorrow," said Dr. Obukhov.

Peter feigned surprise and said, "What a strange coincidence! We are also leaving early morning tomorrow."

"By which flight?" inquired Dr. Obukhov.

"Flight TG101 to London," replied Peter

"Flight TG 101?" repeated Dr. Obukhov. "We are also going by the same flight"

"This flight goes to London. I thought you're going back to Russia," said Peter.

"I have been invited to participate in a conference in London and that is why I'll be going. The Chinese team members are also accompanying me," revealed Dr. Obukhov.

Peter felt relieved at the notion that the Russian did not seem to be aware of their intentions.

"Thanks for taking the trouble of informing me. We shall meet at the airport," he said, while disconnecting the line.

Peter gave a gist of the conversation he just had, to everyone present in the room. Then he looked towards Kim and said, "We may have to use the syringe on Dr. Obukhov if he decides to be naughty!"

"I'll be watching him closely and use it if necessary," he said.

They went for an early dinner of sandwiches, salads and fruit juice, before going to bed. Peter put the alarm in his watch for 23.00 hours.

Chapter 8

Peter and Margaret were woken up from their slumber by the constant buzzing of the alarm. Peter got up and went to the bathroom to get ready for the mission ahead. He was aware that he will have no sleep and relaxation during the next 20 hours. He got dressed and vacated the bathroom for Margaret's use. She came out dressed in her most seductive attire and a facial make-up that could launch a thousand ships! Peter knew that she had a very big role to play in this operation. She has to keep the "cats" away while the "mice" are at play! The "mice" are the operators executing "dragon" and the "cats" are the flight crew in the aircraft who can upset their plans. They went downstairs with their few items of luggage. The most important was Kim's handbag, which he kept glued to his hand. The taxi to take them to the airport was waiting outside. A man, who introduced himself as Kaseem's friend, helped load the luggage and then opened the rear door requesting them to be seated. He also gave Peter a letter from Kaseem and requested him to tear it after reading.

Peter took the letter and read it. The message was as follows: "Co-pilot is Manu, our friend. He will open the pilot's cabin door and go to toilet, exactly 40 minutes after the plane gets airborne"

Peter tore the paper into tiny shreds and threw it out of the window. He looked greatly relieved, as he was worried about the prospect of the pilot's cabin door not opening with the laser torch. They reached the airport after an hour's drive. Peter handed over the bag containing the pistols to Kaseem's friend and, with his help, unloaded the luggage. Kim requested a wheel chair to take him to the luggage screening and security check. He had to convince the authorities that he was an advanced level diabetic patient!

They proceeded to the luggage screening arena, after which they were directed for their boarding passes at the airline counter. They got the passes quickly, as their seats were already booked online. They now proceeded for the security check. This was the most difficult hurdle, thought Peter. Margaret went in first for the security check and came out without any problem, by using all her charms. Peter and Kim followed a little later, as Margaret stood on the other side smiling seductively at the security personnel. They made a perfunctory check of Peter and Kim, while glancing slyly at Margaret. Peter looked back to see if his boys have also got through. He was greatly relieved to see them, which marked the successful execution of the initial part of the operation.

They went to the waiting lounge to await the boarding announcement. Peter and Margaret sat in adjacent seats, while the others were scattered nearby. This was a busy airport and several flights were scheduled for departure during the night. They were watching the sea of humanity in colorful costumes waiting impatiently for their turn. All of a sudden a pair of sturdy hands grabbed Peter's shoulder from behind. Startled, he looked behind to see Dr. Obukhov grinning at him. "Caught you!" He said. "We were looking for both of you, but couldn't see you. Thought you were fast asleep in your hotel and forgot about the flight!"

"Can't afford to miss it. I have to report for work tomorrow. Where are your Chinese comrades?" he asked.

Dr. Obukhov pointed in a particular direction and said, "There they are!"

Aiguo was seated on a seat close to the airlines counter, deeply engrossed with his laptop computer. His wife, Chunhua, was seated next to him, reading a book she had probably bought at the airport bookshop. The other Chinese men and women were seated in the rows behind.

Yelena sat on the seat next to Margaret and complimented her dress. Margaret smiled and returned the compliments. Dr. Obukhov commented, "I hope we can sit next to each other in the plane during the flight. What is your seat number?"

Peter took out his boarding pass and showed it to him.

Dr. Obukhov took out his boarding pass and saw that his seat was many rows behind Peter's. "I am afraid we can't sit together," he lamented. "However, it's good we came to know each other well."

Just then, there was an announcement on the microphone, "Passengers boarding Flight TG-101 to London, are requested to check in at the counter with their boarding passes."

Dr. Obukhov and Yelena got up to join the queue. Peter and Margaret remained seated and decided to join the queue at a later stage.

There was a scramble of passengers to stand in the queue before the counter and gain early entry into the plane. The commotion distracted Aiguo, who looked up with a frown to get a grip of the situation. The long queue evoked an expression of disgust on his face, as he got up lazily, put the laptop in the bag and joined the other passengers. His wife followed him with her handbag. He briefly surveyed the passengers in the queue and found there were many Chinese, Americans, Britons and Indians. The ladies wore scantily clad, bright colored clothes, revealing the latest fashions. The men wore casual summer outfit, in conformity with the hot conditions in Thailand. The queue gradually inched forward and he soon found himself seated inside the plane on a seat next to the aisle. His wife was seated on the adjacent seat. Peter and Margaret were about the last passengers to enter the plane. They went to their seats in the second row. Before sitting he looked around to see his men seated at the appropriate seats.

After sometime Kim got up from his seat and stood on the aisle on the pretext of searching something in his handbag. Sid walked up to him and received a syringe secretly, wrapped in a small plastic bag. The "fasten- your- seatbelt" announcement was made through the intercom and the airline crew walked along the aisle to ensure that the seat position was right and the seat belts were fastened by all the passengers. A few minutes later the Captain's voice came on the line. He introduced himself as Captain Frank Adams and welcomed everybody on board. He said the plane is about to taxi to the main runway in preparation for the lift-off. He gave details about the flight before switching off.

The passengers waited in tense anticipation as the plane taxied on full power till it lifted off the ground towards the sky. After flying for a few minutes it leveled off and the "fasten-your-seatbelt" sign was removed. A loud metallic clang reverberated across the cabin as the passengers unbuckled their respective seatbelts. Kim got up and walked towards the toilet, closely followed by Peter. After Kim came out, Peter entered and found a plastic bag with a syringe.

He went back to his seat and handed the bag to Margaret. Peter kept observing the route map of the flight projected on the TV screen fixed on the back of the seat in the first row. He also saw the time in his watch occasionally. The plane was gradually approaching the border between Thailand and Myanmar

When forty minutes of flight time was about to be completed, the door of the pilot's cabin opened and a short, dark-complexioned man emerged. He stood for a few seconds surveying the passenger cabin, before walking towards the toilet. That was the signal for Sid to get up and stand near the pilot's cabin. Margaret also got up and kept the cabin crew in the vicinity engaged in conversation, which was her specialty. The co-pilot returned and as he was entering the cabin, Sid slipped in along with him. He took out the syringe from his bag and in a flash, injected a portion into the neck of the pilot, who slumped into his seat, after struggling for a few seconds. Sid moved him from his seat into a back seat, with the help of the co-pilot. The transponder was already switched off by the co-pilot, who also put the plane on an auto- pilot mode. He then opened the cabin door again to signal that everything is OK. Peter got up and after ensuring that nobody is watching, lifted the trap door and went below to pull out the circuit breaker for the ACARS system. The plane was now cut off from all communications.

Margaret saw a steward walking towards the pilot's cabin. She immediately diverted his attention by asking for a first-aid box. He went back to respond to the request, giving Peter ample time to come out of the trap door and enter the pilot's cabin. He now used his expertise, as a test pilot to take complete control of the plane. He switched from auto-pilot to manual and raised the flight level to reach 45000 feet. The oxygen masks fell automatically as he used manual depressurization to reduce the cabin pressure. Sid came out of the pilot's cabin and collected the extra oxygen cylinders for the members of his team. After a few minutes the effect of hypoxia began to set in and passengers with crew members began to fall unconscious. Peter had turned the plane into a south-west direction and was flying over the Bay of Bengal Sea, south of the Andaman Islands. The plane was engulfed in pitch darkness with no sign of lights seen anywhere. Peter now plummeted the plane down to an altitude of 5000 feet, during the next twenty minutes and then leveled off. He switched off the lights inside the plane, so that it is not visible from any ship or plane. The headlights were also switched off. The pilot's cabin was lit by a low intensity lamp to read the instruments and the compass.

The plane was now navigated only by the compass and Peter's vast experience. He had flown to Diego Garcia so many times that he had no difficulty in finding its precise direction under any circumstances. After flying for four hours, Peter spotted the lights of the aircraft carrier, which was anchored close to the island. He maneuvered the plane to bring it in alignment with the runway and then put on the headlights to make a perfect landing. After it stopped, it was skillfully taxied to the underground hangar. Now the lights inside the plane were put on, revealing a pathetic scene with passengers lying unconscious on the aisle and the passages between the seats. Some of the passengers were beginning to regain consciousness and muttering unintelligible words. The plane was now taken over by the local men, which included doctors. Peter asked the major-in-charge to transmit the following message to CIA headquarters:

BOMBER ARRIVED WITH SPARES

This is the code to signify that the operation has been successful. Peter and his team were taken to the rest house for food and much needed rest.

Chapter 9

They got up late in the morning and after freshening up, went to the dining room for breakfast. The 'breaking news' in the TV was the disappearance of Flight TG-101 from Bangkok. Various explanations were put forward, some of which were outright ludicrous. The most common explanation was that it crashed in the Bay of Bengal due to mechanical failure. Peter and his team members had a good laugh when they heard it. One reporter suggested that it was hijacked by the Al Qaida, to be used in future bombing missions. A detailed scrutiny was made of the passenger list, by the Thai Government. Two Muslim names were found in the list, with doubtful credentials. Their passports also appeared to be forged. The needle of suspicion was immediately turned on them. It was suggested that they were the hijackers.

After breakfast, they were all taken to the underground hangar to have a look. They were met at the entrance by the Major in-charge, and informed that all the passengers have gained consciousness, except the pilot, who had perhaps, received a rather heavy dose of the medicine. He is being treated by the doctor. He added that the Chinese and Russian computer engineers were segregated from the rest, in accordance with the identities notified by Sid. They were kept in a different chamber in the building. The other passengers were kept in an adjacent chamber with proper facilities of beds and chairs. They were provided food, but most of them refused it. Peter and Margaret took a peep into this chamber and found the passengers were in a dazed state and unable to comprehend the situation. They went to the hangar where the aircraft was kept. In a corner, all the checked-in luggage were kept and adjacent to it, the handbags, mobiles and laptops were kept, tagged with their respective seat numbers. The mobiles were all switched off to remove any chance of anybody identifying the location. The technicians had arrived and the task of dismantling the aircraft had begun.

Margaret had never seen the island of Diego Garcia. Peter volunteered to take her round this beautiful island, with which he was very familiar. He requested an army jeep and took her to the Officer's club. This building sits at the tip of the island on Eclipse Point and has a beautiful view of both, the Indian Ocean and lagoon.

After feasting her eyes with the beautiful sight, Margaret remarked, "I've never seen paradise, but I guess, it must be something like this. Why did you leave such a beautiful place?"

"Well! It's not in my hands. I just have to go where I'm destined to go. Now, I'll take you inside and let you have the taste of one of the finest tropical menu of crabs and fish," he said, leading her to the dining table.

Peter ordered two special menus for brunch and requested the waitress to make it with special care for his guest.

She smiled and returned ten minutes later with two plates of steaming hot stuff, which triggered their olfactory nerves and increased their appetite, to the extent of repeating the order.

"Yeah! I've never tasted anything so delicious!" she remarked.

"Ah! Now I'm sure you will never forget me, because I'm the one who made you taste it," he laughed.

She returned the laugh and suggested a visit to the beach for a swim.

"I have a better idea," he said. "I'll take you for scuba diving. There's no place better than this for this sport."

"Oh! I love it!" she squeaked, as her face lit up.

Peter took her to the beach club where he collected the scuba diving accessories for himself and Margaret. They jumped into the clear waters of the sea and explored the continental shelf with its vegetation and colorful fishes. Their exploration lasted an hour, after which they surfaced and went in the clubhouse to dry them and dress up.

"I've spent the most wonderful evening, Peter! I owe it to you," she said, giving him a flying kiss.

"Thanks! I wish the kiss was nearer to its intended spot," he said, with a twinkle.

On the way back to the rest house, Peter showed her the quarters where he stayed, the gym, the basketball court, the golf course, and finally going past the naval base, where the largest submarine in the US navy is based.

"It's a great place to live. Hardly the place where the aborigines used to stay, a few decades ago," remarked Margaret.

At the rest house Kim was waiting with a message from CIA headquarters that they are to fly to the Qatar air base in a stealth fighter jet in the morning and from there they will proceed to London in a passenger plane, in which their seats have been booked. In London they will get back their old identities, along with passports and other items taken from them. From London they will fly back to Virginia, in a regular passenger airline flight. The passengers of Flight

TG-101 will be taken to the Edwards Air Force base in Nevada, two days later, in a B52 bomber, via service halts in Qatar Air Force base and Lajes Field Air base in Portugal. He will accompany them along with a few others.

Peter and Margaret bid good-bye to Kim and went to their room. They had early dinner and retired for a good night's sleep. In the morning the doorbell rang and Peter went to investigate. He found Kim standing at the door, waiting to drive them to the runway where the stealth fighter was kept in readiness. Peter and Margaret got dressed quickly and accompanied Kim to the parked jeep. Kim had thoughtfully brought some sandwiches for them to munch on the way. They reached the Stealth fighter and alighted from the jeep to board it. Before boarding, Peter thanked Kim and said, "We'll meet again shortly in Nevada, perhaps, in our original identities. I hope you'll recognize us. We pray that you recover from your diabetes very soon."

Kim laughed loudly and said, "Who can forget this operation and the people who were associated with me!"

Peter sat on the pilot's chair, with Margaret acting as his co-pilot, and took off en route for Qatar.

On their arrival at Qatar they were met by the base commander, a tall burly man, with a moustache matching his volume. He took them in a jeep to the waiting lounge for some refreshments. He motioned a pilot to get the plane taxied to its hangar, before sitting down for a chat with Peter and Margaret. "I was in your squadron in the Iraq campaign," he said looking towards Peter.

"Yeah, I felt so! But I couldn't quite place you, because you have put on a lot of weight," he replied.

He laughed and said, "I went after my father who was also in the army. He was slim when joined, but bloated when he took his discharge ten years later."

"What does he do now?" inquired Peter.

"We have a family business in Minnesota. He looks after it. My wife and brother also stay there," he replied.

He excused himself and returned after some time with an envelope containing two airline tickets.

"These are your tickets by flight QR-015 to London, which leaves at 14.50 hours and reaches London at 20.25, just in time for dinner. You will be received by an official of the embassy, who will guide you thereafter," he said, as he handed over the tickets to Peter.

They were taken to the Hamad International airport, where they completed all the check-in formalities and waited in the lounge until the boarding for the flight was announced. They boarded the plane and were guided to their seats by beautiful air hostesses in their attractive maroon colored uniforms with matching head gears.

Once seated, Peter heaved a sigh of relief and whispered mischievously close to Margaret's ear, "This is our last trip together as husband and wife. Let's make the best of it!"

"Oh, shut up! What exactly do you want to do?" retorted Margaret with a frown.

"Nothing objectionable, I promise! Just a little romantic talk, maybe an exchange of a kiss or two," stuttered Peter.

"There'll plenty of time for all this in Virginia," replied she, with a smile.

"Well! Once you are in Virginia, Richard will take over and you'll be entirely under his command all the time," retorted Peter.

"I'll be busy, but we can still meet once a week or perhaps a month and spend some quality time together," reasoned she.

"A week is too long a waiting time and a month is out of reckoning!" remarked Peter.

"OK! Right now I may have to go to Nevada to act as an interpreter in the interrogation process. Why don't you also come there and help me?" advised Margaret.

"There are many helpers available. I may not get any chance!" lamented Peter.

"Why not? You have been the key person in the execution of 'dragon.' You must have a 'say' in these proceedings, too!" justified Margaret.

"My job was only to pilot the aircraft to Diego Garcia, safely. Once that is done, I'm an expendable commodity!" said Peter.

"Nonsense!" said Margaret angrily. "A man's qualities cannot be gauged by just one act. Executing an operation requires skills in planning, organizing and motivating the other members of the team, which cannot be ignored by anyone heading the organization."

At that moment, the air hostess stood on the aisle besides Peter, with her trolley containing beverages and asked if he wanted tea, coffee, or any other drink.

"Two hot coffee, please!" he said, looking towards Margaret for confirmation of the order.

Margaret nodded and the hostess poured hot coffee from a pot into two paper cups and gave it to them. Peter was enjoying the coffee and engrossed in his own thoughts, when he passed away into dreamland. Margaret was already in the process of taking forty winks with her eyes shut.

Peter was woken by an announcement by the Captain. "We are now descending over London and expected to land in thirty minutes. Passengers are requested to fasten the seat belts," blared the microphone. Margaret also woke up and began fastening her seat belt. "I completely lost sense of time," she remarked.

"So did I!" rejoined Peter. "I was just dreaming of the good times we spent together when the announcement killed my dream."

Margaret smiled and glanced out of the window. There was still enough sunlight to see the buildings in London as the plane descended towards Heathrow airport. The wheels soon touched the runway and the plane taxied to a halt in front of the aerobridge for disembarkation. Peter and Margaret walked briskly towards the conveyor belt for collecting their checked-in luggage. As they came out of the exit gate an official of the embassy met them and introduced himself as James Austin. He said he was to take them to their hotel and hand over a suitcase.

Margaret recognized him as a CIA operator and said, "Hello James! How are you?"

James replied, "Well, thanks! I received a message from headquarters yesterday, to give you these papers. How was your trip?"

Margaret introduced Peter to him and said their trip was fine, but now they are eager to go home. He reached the hotel and took them to their separate, adjacent rooms, booked under their real identities. They all entered Peter's room and sat on the sofa. He opened the suitcase and took out an envelope. "These are your original passports, credit cards, driving license and wallet. From now onwards you are to use your real identity," he said. He gave Margaret her purse containing all the documents. He further informed them that their clothes are in the suitcase, which he is leaving behind.

"Your flight to Washington leaves tomorrow from Heathrow at 11.30 hours. I shall come to pick you at 9.30 hours. Is there anything else I can do?" he asked.

Herman (alias Peter) and Della (alias Margaret) thanked him and said they would be expecting him next day at 9.30 hours, after wishing him good-night.

"It's a great relief to be known once again by our original identity," said Herman, after the departure of James.

"Yeah! The fake identity made me feel like a shady character," agreed Della.

Herman switched on the TV and heard the news channel with great interest. The major part of the news coverage concerned the disappearance of Flight TG-101, flying from Bangkok to London. It said that an exhaustive search operation has begun over the Bay of Bengal Sea, by the Thai, Indian, Chinese and Russian Air Force and Navy personnel, on the presumption that the plane had crashed into the sea. The Thai defense minister was addressing a press conference in which a journalist asked about the Muslim passengers with fake passports being associated with the disappearance. The minister answered that investigations, with the help of Interpol, did not reveal that they had any connection with any known terrorist organization. They were found to be unemployed youths who wanted to go to London for jobs and possible asylum.

To another question whether it was a case of hijacking, the minister answered that so far, no demands, either monetary or political, have been made from any organization. So, the chances of a hijack seem to be slender. However, he did not rule it out completely. Another question concerned the failure of the tracking system in locating the position of the aircraft. The minister replied that the electronic signaling systems in the plane were either switched off, or it was not working, due to which no signals were received by the tracking devices.

Herman smiled and said, "Only the last answer appears to be closest to the truth. The others are miles off the track. They are still completely in the dark about the location of the plane."

Della agreed and added, "It shows the complete success of 'operation dragon'!"

Herman and Della went together for dinner, after which they returned to their respective rooms.

"In case you feel lonely, you can call me," Herman told mischievously while parting.

"I'm used to sleeping alone. So I don't feel lonely. Anyway thanks for volunteering!" Della replied.

"In case I feel lonely, can I call you?" asked Herman with a smile.

"Definitely not!" replied Della sternly and entered her room.

Herman got up early next morning and got dressed for breakfast. He switched on the TV to hear further developments on Flight TG-101. In the meantime Della also joined him in his room, dressed up for breakfast. The latest news was that satellite pictures showed some parts floating in the southern Indian Ocean, which appeared to be the parts of a plane. The Australian Government was requested to send their Navy to explore the floating objects. They acceded to the request and sent their naval ship to the coordinates shown by the satellite pictures, but found the objects were not plane parts.

"There goes another hypothesis down the drain!" Herman said sarcastically.

"You have sent them on a wild goose chase," added Della, smiling.

They went down together for breakfast, carrying their luggage with them. They deposited the luggage at the reception counter and checked themselves out. They had breakfast and were waiting in the lobby for James to arrive. He arrived at 9.30 sharp and walked straight to the elevator. Herman followed behind him and seized him before he entered the elevator.

"We have been waiting for you. We have brought our luggage and checked out of our rooms," said Herman.

James looked pleased and led them towards the car he had brought to take them to the airport.

On the way he asked them, "Have you checked your documents and found them to be in order?" he asked.

"Yes, everything is OK!" replied Della, on behalf of both of them.

They entered the car and were on the way to the airport. After the usual drill, they got their boarding cards and were waiting in the hall for the announcement to board the plane.

"You know, Della, it surprises me to hear in the news that the USA Government has not actively joined the search for Flight TG-101, barring the expression of sympathy for the loss," Herman said looking towards Della.

"What's surprising in it? They can't possibly draw the attention of the search party to Diego Garcia," she replied.

"I understand their predicament, but being the most advanced nation in terms of electronic devices and the size of the Naval and Air force, everybody expect them to contribute actively in the search. Their symbolic gesture may give rise to the suspicion that they are behind the disappearance," Herman argued.

"OK, what would you have done if you were the President of USA?" Della asked.

"Well! Since you are bestowing upon me this honor, I will tell you what I will do. I will first plant a story about the involvement of Al Qaida in this hijacking. They want to use this plane for a9/11 type of attack on some important landmark and they have hidden it in some remote island. Then I will create some fake intercepts of messages to substantiate the story and whip up a frenzy against the Al Qaida, through the help of our friendly media. The CIA is very good in doing such things on behalf of the President. Then I will have a Boeing 777 plane stationed in some remote Atlantic island and have it bombed to demonstrate that we mean business. In this way, I will kill two birds with one stone. First, I will isolate Al Qaida in the eyes of the world and second, I will execute operation 'dragon' without anyone knowing about it!" said Herman.

Della clapped softly and said, "Bravo! You should become the President of USA. I'm sure the CIA will be a more useful tool under your leadership."

Herman smiled at the compliment and said, "Today, the world is divided into power blocks, each block trying to prove that it is stronger than the others. In the process, innocent people are made pawns and have to pay a heavy price."

"Awl! Don't ever say these things in the corridors of power. You'll be sent to Guantanamo and nobody will ever hear about you!" warned Della.

"I know! I have also been a part of this organization and committed many heinous crimes in the name of protecting the world against all evil," admitted Herman.

Chapter 10

The announcement to board the plane was made. Herman and Della got up and proceeded to the boarding counter. They soon occupied their seats in the plane. After half an hour they became airborne en route for Washington. They spent most of the time sleeping, until it was time to descend over the Dulles International airport, Washington D.C. It was a bright sunny evening when they came out of the airport. They were received by Richard Crawley and Harold Stacey. They were seated in the waiting car, which sped towards the CIA headquarters in Virginia.

They maintained a stoic silence for the first ten minutes, after which Harold turned round and extended his hand towards Herman. "This is for a work well done," he said. Herman smiled in acknowledgement. They reached the CIA headquarters and walked straight to Richard's room, where John was already waiting in anticipation of their arrival.

John was the first to walk up to him and shook his hands. He said, "I had already told you, you'll not receive any applause for success in this operation and we'll disown you if you fail. Very harsh words indeed! Any young man would feel extremely discouraged to hear such words from the head of an organization. But, I know you are a hardened soldier and trained to hear these words. This is reality. We're like scavengers who work day and night, all seasons, to keep the city clean, but get no rewards. If they don't work for one day, immediately complaints, abuses pile up against them for not doing their duty. I am extremely proud of what you've done, but I can't express it in public. Nobody should know who is the key person and organization behind 'operation dragon.' Honestly, there was no other way to prevent this catastrophe. If disaster strikes us, it will strike the other countries, as well. The people who are perpetrators of this crime, will also become victims someday, but, by then, the entire world will be in chaos. The most that I can do is to sanction a paid holiday for a week, to you and your family, to any place of your choice. You can consider this as your reward."

Herman thanked him and said, "Sir, I am proud to be chosen for this operation, even though, I knew the consequences of failure. As you rightly said, I took up this job of a scavenger to keep the city clean for others. I did not do it for getting an award, but for the thrill. The thrill of doing something for others kept me focused on my mission. I am glad that you have acknowledged my merits, at least in your heart, if not publicly. I must also acknowledge the help and cooperation of all the members of my team, without which it would not have been possible to carry out the operation. I appeal to you for considering an appropriate award for them, too. Lastly, I cannot think of enough praise for my 'co-pilot' Della, who not only helped me control the plane in rough weather, but, also ensured that I never lost sight of my target."

John embraced him, patting him on the back and said, "Maybe, thirty years hence, when the secret documents are declassified, somebody will read about your heroic deeds and applaud you in person, or posthumously. A new generation of Americans will express their gratitude to you for saving the country from disaster. I may not be present to see this happen. I greatly appreciate your acknowledgement of the help received from your team members in the right spirit of camaraderie. This is what makes a great leader. I shall certainly consider an appropriate reward for them, too."

It was now Richard's turn to shake his hands and applaud him, followed by Harold, once again. Conspicuous by her absence, was Della, who had gone to her room and got busy in her secretarial work. John went back to his room, leaving Richard, Harold and Herman to discuss the repercussions of 'operation dragon.'

Richard called Della on the intercom and asked her to bring the file on 'operation dragon.' She entered the room a few minutes later with the file and said, "this also contains the press reports about the disappearance of Flight TG -101.'

He glanced over the file for a few minutes and said, "The Thai authorities have still no inkling of the location of the missing aircraft and are under the belief that it crashed somewhere in the Indian Ocean. The Chinese Government is pressurizing them to expedite the search on the missing plane, as many Chinese were in the list of passengers, who had expertise in Computer technology. The Russian authorities are conducting their own investigations through their spy satellites. The KGB did attempt to cross check the fake identities of some of our operators in 'operation dragon', but have not been able to obtain any significant information. Sooner or later, they will learn the truth about our secret operation, but, before that happens, we must learn everything about their project and also suppress it from progressing any further."

Harold enquired, "When will the cross examination of the Chinese and Russian computer engineers begin?"

"They are being transported to Edwards Air Force base, today, from where they will be taken to the Nevada Test and Training Range. Our software experts are already in Nevada, to sift their laptops for any information of value," replied Richard.

It was becoming time for dinner and Richard requested Della to take Herman to the guest house. In the car, Della spoke first, "I have been assigned the duty of assisting in the interrogation of the Chinese and Russian computer experts. I shall be leaving for Nevada tomorrow and you are also coming with me. Your job will be to test fly a new stealth fighter jet which has been designed."

"How come I am also assigned a job in Nevada?" he inquired.

"Well! You made me your 'co-pilot' for 'operation dragon.' So, at some point of time you have to be my 'co-pilot' and assist me in my operations. Fair enough!" replied Della.

"Fair enough!" agreed Herman. "But, how did you know that I've made you my 'co-pilot'? You were not present during the briefing!"

"It's my job to know everything that is going on in my boss's room, even during my absence," said Della.

They both enjoyed a little laughter. "Here's your guest house. You can have dinner and go to bed early. I'll come in the morning after breakfast to pick you up," said Della as she stopped the car.

"Won't you come in and share dinner with me?" asked Herman.

"I'd love to..., but I have some important tasks to attend to. Some other time. OK," replied Della and accelerated her car, after blowing a kiss in his direction.

Chapter 11

It was midnight and the giant B-52 bomber stood on the tarmac in Diego Garcia, awaiting its load of very special "bombs," which are to be dropped only at the Edwards Air Force base, Nevada, in USA. This bomber was modified with chairs, attached seat belts, and a good ventilation system, to accommodate around 240 personnel. It was also provided with 8 toilets and two kitchenettes to store food packets and water for distribution. The plane was being readied with food packets and water.

A convoy of military trucks arrived near the bomber ladder which connected the entrance of the plane. As each truck stood before the base of the ladder in turn, the civilians inside the truck were disgorged and asked to climb the ladder to the entrance. Soon all the civilians were seated in the plane along with a dozen army personnel and four doctors, under the charge of Major Paul Scott. The plane was divided into two compartments, one small and the other large. The computer engineers were put in the smaller compartment, while the rest were accommodated in the larger.

The plane taxied to take off en route for Qatar air base. The passengers were still dazed, but fit enough to be transported by plane. Some passengers were given sleep injections to keep them quiet. The plane touched down at Qatar, four hours later. It was still dark outside. The plane was re-fuelled, stacked with food packets and water. After a 30 minute halt it took off again for Lajes Field air base in Portugal. It is located in the North Atlantic Ocean on the island of Terceira, which is one of the nine inhabited islands of the Azores archipelago. It is about 2300 miles east of Washington D.C. The plane touched down in Portugal after a five-hour flight. Here the pilot and co-pilot were changed. The doctors kept a constant vigil on the conditions of the passengers. The usual routine of re-fuelling, stacking were completed. The plane took off after a forty minute halt en route for its last destination, Edwards air force base, USA. It flew for six hours before it touched down at the base.

It was still dark outside and dawn was just emerging in the distant horizon. A convoy of army trucks was kept ready and as the passengers alighted, they were asked to board the trucks. When all the passengers had alighted, the convoy took off to an unknown destination across the desert. After an hour's travel, they arrived at the center which will be their home during the coming months. It is known as 'Area 51' which is off bound to visitors and heavily guarded. The only inhabitants are the team of defense personnel, doctors, psychiatrists, nurses and scientists, who are bound by the secrecy clause not to reveal the functions of the center to the outside world. The passengers of the B-52 were quickly rehabilitated to their respective quarters, under the watchful eyes of the Director, Colonel Sam Stewart. The computer engineers were kept in a different location for being interrogated by the experts from CIA, while the others were to be brainwashed by the team of psychiatrists, in order to erase the events of the last couple of weeks from their memories.

The team from the CIA headquarters arrived the next day, which included Della and Herman. They were housed in the Block meant for visiting experts. Herman shared a room with the chief interrogator, Dr. Alistair Corsin.

By way of introduction, Herman talked about his town of birth and the school where he had his education. He requested Alistair to divulge his brief bio-data and was surprised to note that they both had their schooling in the same town in Texas. This was a major factor to draw them closer to each other. Herman was interested in knowing how he would interrogate the two different groups of people.

Alistair explained, "There are two basic types of interrogation techniques that are employed in the army to interrogate prisoners. One is 'elicitation' and the other, 'brainwashing.' Prisoners exploited through elicitation must retain sufficient clarity of thought to be able to give coherent, factual information. In the case of the computer engineers, we want them to tell us clearly what they are doing. So we employ this technique. In brainwashing, on the other hand, we attack the clarity of thought of the subject, so that he is confused. He then depends on the interrogator to get clues about his thoughts. The best clues are the internal reactions to the pressures he undergoes."

The next day the interrogation process was scheduled to begin. A few glass cubicles with a table and three chairs were arranged. One chair was for the subject and the other two on the opposite side were for the interrogators. A powerful light shone on the subject and the table. The glass panes were bullet proof and sound proof. The subject cannot see anyone on the other side of the glass pane, but people on the other side can see him and also his camera view, as well as hear his voice through a microphone system. The proceedings were recorded.

Herman had interrogated some POWs in Iraq and wanted to see how these interrogations were conducted. He decided to accompany Alistair to the interrogation room. On the way he met Della, hurrying to the venue with a file.

"Are you going to interrogate the Russian today?" he asked her.

"There'll be a regular interrogator inside the cubicle. I'll be sitting outside the glass window, watching the proceedings and, maybe, ask a few questions in Russian. Why don't you help me frame the questions?" she asked, with a smile.

"I'll be glad to! In fact that is where I'm going now. My room-mate, Alistair, is the chief interrogator," he replied.

They all proceeded to the interrogation room. The first to be interrogated was Dr. Obukhov. He was brought inside the first cubicle and seated. He still looked a bit dazed after the long ordeal. After some time, Dr. Alistair Corsin entered and seated himself on the opposite chair. He introduced himself and extended his hand for a handshake. "How are you feeling today?" he asked.

Dr. Obukhov made no effort to answer the question and gave a blank stare. Alistair took out a cigarette from his case and offered it to him, " Here you are, this sometimes makes you feel better!"Dr. Obukhov grabbed it and began puffing after Alistair lighted it with his lighter. "Would you mind discussing with me a few items of great importance?" he asked.

"I have nothing to discuss with you," he said in a gruff voice.

"I know you're very angry after this strenuous flight. It's not our fault," said Alistair as politely as possible.

"Angry!" he shouted. "I have been kidnapped by the CIA and you have been sent by them to discuss with me!"

"Now ! You're unnecessarily blaming the CIA. Why would they kidnap you? Have you done anything to arouse their anger?" Alistair asked.

"The CIA is a terrorist organization specialized in kidnapping," he said in Russian.

Della translated it into English and said it in the microphone, which was picked up by Alistair in his earphone.

"I understood what you've said in Russian. If the CIA were really a terrorist organization, as you say, then why did they not kidnap your President Putin, who has been critical of the Americans? Why did they kidnap you? Are you related to him?" he asked.

"Putin is critical of Americans because they interfere in the internal matters of Russia," he said angrily.

"But, this does not answer the question why, you think, the CIA has kidnapped you?"

"Who else would kidnap a plane load of innocent people?"

"That's right! Who would kidnap a plane load of innocent people? Are you sure all the people in the plane were innocent?"

"Do you think we are all crooks in the plane?"

"Why would the CIA kidnap crooks? They will have more of a nuisance value."

"They want to increase their number. Every terrorist gang needs to recruit more people to increase the number."

"They can do the same by recruiting fresh people, pay them handsomely and train them. Why will they kidnap crooks?"

"I was suggesting that you think we are crooks. Actually we are all respectable people engaged in a respectable profession."

"What is your profession, Dr. Obukhov?"

"You might have already seen it in my passport. I am a teacher in a school."

"What subject do you teach?"

"I teach computer science."

"What is your qualification Dr. Obukhov?

"I have a Ph. d in computer science from Moscow University."

"Which branch of computer science have you specialized in?"

"Software development on cloud structuring."

"That is a very recent development. How come you are only a school teacher with this qualification?"

"I like teaching school children and that is why I chose this job."

"You know Dr. Obukhov, any person with that qualification in this country will earn five times more as salary!"

"High salary has never been the sole motive in my life."

"Do you earn something more as a consultant, somewhere?"

"I don't need to do it. I'm happy with my salary and live quite comfortably."

"What is your recent project?"

"I am teaching my students the basic science of software development."

"Apart from regular teaching, don't you do any research?"

"I don't get any time outside my regular curriculum."

Alistair opened a file before him and said, "Dr. Obukhov, I have before me the title of the paper you presented at the conference in London in 2011, organized by the International Computer Society. The title suggests the result of a very advanced research on a subject which is way beyond the boundaries of your school curriculum. How do you explain that?"

Dr. Obukhov kept quiet for a moment and then replied, "I don't have to explain it. It was a part of my doctoral thesis which I thought of presenting at the conference."

"You are lying again, Dr. Obukhov! I have the synopsis of your doctoral thesis and nowhere in it is this topic mentioned. It is a very recent development, maybe, about two to three years ago, much later after the date of submission of your thesis."

Dr. Obukhov kept silent.

Alistair kept up the pressure, "Dr. Obukhov, I am asking again. This is research of a very advanced nature. For whom are you working?"

Dr. Obukhov feigned to get angry. "I am free to do any research I want. I don't have to give any explanation to anyone!"

"You are not free to do any research which is aimed at harming other countries. I want to know which organization is supporting your research and how much are they paying you?"

Dr. Obukhov remained silent and turned his head.

"The saying, 'silence is golden' does not work here. We can find out everything about this project. If you confide the details to me earlier, I'll consider you my friend and try to help you. Do you know, the people who are supporting you in this project are very dangerous and have no sanctity for human life. You will become disposable as soon as their work is done."

Dr. Obukhov still remained silent.

"OK Dr. Obukhov, we break here for lunch. When we meet again, I hope, you'll be in a better frame of mind and cooperate," said Alistair before leaving the room. Dr. Obukhov was taken by the security men to the dining hall.

Herman and Della also went together for lunch in the guest house canteen. They selected a corner table and sat. Alistair walked in and Herman motioned him to join them. He introduced him to Della, but they seemed to know each other. Alistair greeted them and sat down.

"Your interrogation was excellent. You almost cornered him to submission," remarked Herman.

"It's like a game of tennis. One who can place his shots better can wrong foot his opponent and win the match. These Russians are very stubborn. They know that sooner or later, they will be tracked by the KGB, who are ruthless. Their only punishment is death," replied Alistair with a grin.

At that moment another computer software expert, Dr. Allen Grant, known to Alistair, walked in. Alistair called him and introduced him to everyone. He asked him whether he had succeeded in opening Dr. Obukhov's laptop.

"Yes, after a lot of efforts I managed to identify the password. It was written very cleverly and difficult to decode. There were a lot of things written in Russian, but the English texts I could follow. They were methods of setting a backdoor in windows, so that it can be accessed anytime even if the passwords are changed," he said.

"Fine!" remarked Alistair. "Have you brought the laptop? We have a Russian here who can tell you what the Russian texts are," he said, pointing towards Della.

He took out the laptop from his bag and placed it on the table. He opened windows and pushed it towards Della. She studied the texts for sometimes and told Allen, "These are syntax commands and gives the net user's account name in Russian."

Allen then told Alistair many other important texts which he found and noted it in a notebook, which he gave to him. After taking lunch, followed by a little siesta in the lounge, they walked back to the interrogation center and occupied their places. Dr. Obukhov was already seated.

"I hope you feel better after lunch, Dr. Obukhov," he said.

Dr. Obukhov shrugged his shoulders and said with a frown, "There is nothing to feel better."

"So, you don't want to cooperate and remain adamant."

Dr. Obukhov remained silent and non-committal.

"OK! Then let me tell you that we have succeeded in opening the password of your laptop and gone through all the texts, programs and including those written in Russian. We've also found some nude photographs of a few women. You know what that means?"

Dr. Obukhov's face turned crimson and he appeared less adamant. "What are you up to? Do you want to blackmail me? I will not say anything."

"We are not in the habit of blackmailing. Besides, what do we get by blackmailing you? You are hardly in a position to give us any ransom. I am just thinking what will happen if your bosses come to know that you are passing on the secret work to unwanted quarters!"

"OK! What do you want to know?"

"We don't want to know anything. You have to tell us what you are doing and who is funding your work."

"What difference will it make?"

"It will make a difference. Now we will have an authentic version of what we already know. We can also seek certain clarifications."

Dr. Obukhov thought for a while and said, "There are other people of different nationalities involved in this project. I have to consult them."

"You don't have to worry about that. We know who are the people involved and their nationalities. Aiguo, his wife Chunhua and four of their colleagues from China, Yelena and yourself from Russia. All you have to do is tell us the details of your project and to what stage you have reached. You have to also tell us who is funding your project."

Dr. Obukhov was surprised to hear all the names from them. He asked, "How did you know all the names? We were working very secretly and thought nobody suspected us."

"That is the biggest mistake you made, 'working very secretly.' When somebody is covertly cautious, he invites suspicion, which leads to discreet inquiry and finally the names are out!"

"Any revelation from my side will endanger the lives of the other people involved with me."

"Don't worry about them. They are very safe here with us and will continue to be so, unless you do something indiscreet."

"What do you mean by 'indiscreet'?"

"It means if you don't cooperate and do the things we want you to do, we shall have to disclose your presence here. Then you know what might happen."

"Can I talk with my other colleagues?"

"As a rule we don't allow discussions between people who are under interrogation. But, if you tell us the details of the project and the identity of the fund supplier, we may allow you to meet your other colleagues."

Dr. Obukhov was deep in thought, when Della decided to speak to him in Russian, from her seat behind the glass. She told him to do as told and reap the benefits of a good life here, free from the clutches of the KGB.

"Who is that?" asked Dr. Obukhov.

"Oh1 She is a very good researcher who was once working in Russia under the direction of the KGB like you. She then decided to switch allegiance and work for us. Now, she is a senior scientist working here and enjoying all the benefits of high perks, freedom and safety."

"Did you kidnap her, too and interrogated her like me?"

"No! She came on her own and took her own decision at the right time."

"What is her name? I think I have heard her voice before."

"You'll meet her as soon as you take a decision to work for us. She'll herself come and meet you."

Dr. Obukov finally disclosed the details of his work and revealed the funding body to be the Department of Mathematics, under the Russian Academy of Sciences and recommended by the KGB. It was a joint program with the Chinese Academy of Sciences. He said that the project is in the final stages and there are still some problems to be overcome. He signed a document agreeing to work in the USA and apply his research towards improving the data communication networks. He was allowed to meet Yelena and discuss the matter with her. At first she was reluctant to leave Russia and work here, but later she agreed to join Dr. Obukhov. She was, however, apprehensive about the fate of her relatives in Russia, particularly her parents. She was told that once she is given permanent residency permit, she can call them over to stay with her.

The Chinese computer engineer, Aiguo was not cooperating with the interrogator. Alistair and Della were requested to help. Alistair went inside the cubicle and Della sat outside looking through the window.

Alistair began, "Aiguo, I thought you were very sensible like most Chinese scientists I know. Why are you making things difficult for yourself?"

Aiguo looked sternly at him and said, "I will not cooperate with you. You people are thugs."

"Aiguo, if we were thugs, your friend would not cooperate with us. He has agreed to work with us and accepted us as his friend."

Alistair showed him the signed document of Dr. Obukhov.

"I don't follow him. He can do whatever he wants. I will not work with you," yelled Aiguo.

"You disappoint me, Aiguo! We have unlocked the safe password of your laptop and also your e-mails and read most of the incriminating contents. You don't expect me to tell you about those contents!"

Aiguo was silent and looked at the table, without any expression.

"Tell me who funded your project?"

Aiguo again kept silent.

"We have come to know that the funding agency is the Chinese Academy of Sciences."

"I am not going to tell you anything. You are all thugs."

"We have evidence to show that the aim of this joint project with the Russian scientists was to disrupt our data network and ensure that our computer network crashes. You call us 'thugs', but we don't go about disrupting essential services of other countries, through the illegal use of computer software, which you are doing. You know, if we bring this to the notice of the International body, your funding agencies will all back out and disown you. Ultimately, you will be proclaimed a 'thug' for indulging in illegal activities and sentenced for life. Do you want this to happen?"

Aiguo looked confused and was in two minds.

"I was not aware about the purpose of the project. I was just doing what my boss wanted."

"How can you say this? You are a responsible computer engineer and have designed a software whose aim is to interfere with our commands to the computer and data networks. You have also done some trial experiments to test the efficacy of your software. Who will believe you, particularly when your own country does not support you?"

Aiguo now clearly looked worried. Alistair wanted to seize this opportunity and looked to Della for support.

Della spoke in Chinese, "You should follow Dr. Obukhov and do the right thing. Once the matter leaks to the international forums, your country will disown all responsibilities and claim you did it on your own.

No country will want to be seen as officially embroiled in illegal activities, before the international community."

Aiguo seemed to have recognized the voice, "Is that you, Mrs. Margaret Morris? You have also been kidnapped along with us!"

Della answered with a chuckle, "Yes, they have locked me here and won't let me go!"

He looked towards Alistair and asked, "What have I to do? But, you must let Mrs. Margaret and her husband go. They have nothing to do with this."

"You just sign this undertaking and become our friend. You can also talk to your wife and ensure that she also signs it. Yes, we shall definitely let Mrs. Margaret and her husband go. We have found out they are innocent!"

Alistair and the others accompanying him, looked relieved at solving the case of the software engineers. Della expressed satisfaction with the fact that there wasn't much opposition. Perhaps, it was Alistair's magic that did the trick! He laughed and said, "They were basically very intelligent men and knew the repercussions of what they were doing. It did not take long to convince them. The other members of the software team should follow their leader and join us soon."Herman had gone to the test center to inspect the newly designed stealth fighter jet which he was to test fly the next day. They proceeded to the guest house for dinner.

Chapter 12

Diego Garcia 2 April 2013

The Boeing 777 plane that had brought the passengers of Flight TG-101, from Bangkok to this place on 19 March, was not seen anywhere in the underground hangar. It was dismantled part-by-part and stacked along the side walls. The avionic instruments were first disconnected from the power system in the plane and then deactivated, so that they don't send any signals, using the instrument's internal power system. The plane's body, including the tail, was then ripped into pieces of convenient sizes, using powerful sawing machines. The chairs were taken out and arranged in groups of twenty chairs. The internal wires were cut and rolled into bundles – almost four kilometers in length. The giant compressors of the jet engine were dismantled. All the dismantled parts were stacked in big wooden boxes, with the help of cranes. The dismantling process had been going on, day and night, during the last fortnight. Only a few defense personnel in the base were entrusted with this onerous task. Two of the army personnel, Lt. Will Tucson and Lt. Alan Murphy, who had been a part of the "operation dragon" team, stayed back to oversee the dismantling operations.

The giant Lockheed C-5 Galaxy cargo plane was requisitioned to transport the remains of the Boeing 777 plane to an undisclosed destination for its final resting place. Will was at a loss to understand how this giant cargo plane will land on the small airstrip in the island. Alan had flown in this plane earlier while transporting tanks to the Gulf arena.

He came to his rescue and said, "The C-5 has been designed to carry unusually large and heavy cargo and can take off and land in relatively short distances. It has two openings for cargo loading, one at the front and the other at the rear. It can be loaded and off loaded at the same time. Both nose and rear doors open the full width and height of the cargo compartment, allowing drive-through loading and unloading of wheeled and tracked vehicles."

"How do we lift such heavy cargo to the level of the cargo floor and is there a separate compartment for the personnel accompanying the cargo?" he asked

"A 'kneeling' landing gear system lowers the aircraft's cargo floor to the truck-bed height. The compartment for the personnel accompanying the cargo is located in the aircraft's upper deck. It is self-contained with a gallery, two lavatories and 73 passenger seats," replied Alan. "The Galaxy also has sophisticated communications equipment and a triple inertial navigational system, making it nearly self-sufficient. It can operate without using ground-based navigational aids."

The C-5 Galaxy arrived at night and parked on the tarmac. A convoy of trucks stood in front of the underground hangar. The cranes loaded the big boxes one-by-one on the trucks. After all the trucks were loaded, they left for the location of the C-5 plane. The kneeling landing gear system was employed to lower the aircraft's cargo floor to the truck bed height. The trucks were stationed in front of the front cargo opening and the boxes were pushed into the cargo hold, where the plane's cranes took over and placed them at the appropriate places. After all the boxes were loaded, the front opening was closed and the plane was readied to take = off.

It was well past midnight and pitch dark outside. The faint light of the stars revealed the vast expanse of the

Indian Ocean, giving it a grotesque appearance. Eight army personnel boarded the plane, along with Will and Alan. The plane veered in the direction of the southern Indian Ocean. It flew towards the deepest part of the Ocean, which was free of the shipping lanes. After flying for about an hour, the pilot informed that the area for the drop has come. He came down to a level of about 200 feet above the surface of the water. The rear door opened and the first box on the line was pushed towards it. It tumbled out of the door and hurtled speedily towards the sea. A few seconds later a loud splash was heard and a circular foam of water was seen. The box disappeared into oblivion. The plane had advanced ahead by a couple of kilometers. The second box was now pushed. It was followed by all the boxes in quick succession, till the cargo hold had become empty. The plane now gained height and turned towards Diego Garcia. As it approached the island the first streaks of dawn was visible in the horizon and the most beautiful sight of a sunrise soon followed.

The men had returned after performing the last rites of what was once a magnificent flying machine, the Boeing 777. It now lay thousands of fathoms below the surface of the Indian Ocean, where it can never be discovered. Its beautiful body was dissected into parts and strewn over an area of thousands of square kilometers in the dark abyss of the ocean. The chapter on one of the most daring crimes in history, sponsored by a nation, will remain buried forever. A short message was sent to CIA headquarters:

WWIIBOMB DEFUSED

This was the code for saying that the Flight TG 101 plane was dismantled and disposed of.

Chapter 13

CIA Headquarters, July 2, 2013

John called a meeting with the Heads of the two most important departments, viz., Richard, from the Intelligence department and Harold from the National Clandestine Services department, to discuss the aftermath of the operation dragon. He requested Harold to give his report.

He got up and inserted a few slides into the overhead projector, before reading out the report. The Boeing 777 plane used in Flight TG – 101 has been totally dismantled in Diego Garcia, as shown by the following slides. He presented the slides one after another, depicting the different stages of demolitions. The loading operation was done during the night when it was pitch dark on the runway. The floodlights were switched off to enable the operation to be performed in complete darkness. Only a flashlight was used inside the plane to facilitate loading. The plane departed on April 2 to the Central Indian Ocean, where it is the deepest. Well past midnight, the loaded boxes were dropped in quick succession from a height of about 200 feet above the ocean surface. The dropped boxes spread over an area of around 10 sq. kilometers. There is no evidence of any eye witnesses, or anybody suspecting foul play.

"Good work," remarked John. "Now there is no physical evidence that the Americans are involved in the hijacking of Flight TG-101. Are you sure that there are no islanders who can reveal the details."

"Nobody has seen the plane landing, as it was immediately taken to the underground hangar. The only persons who have seen it are those involved in the dismantling operations and they are trusted people. There are so many landings and take offs, that people don't bother about these."

"OK, your turn, Richard!" he said turning towards Richard.

"We have been closely monitoring the press reports and the interviews given by politicians of different countries, since the disappearance of Flight TG-101. No one has come even close to the actual fact. The nearest version was that of a BBC correspondent, who has speculated that the plane was hijacked and taken to an unknown place by some terrorist. He has not identified the terrorist organization. Most of the views have inferred that it had crashed into the sea and there are no survivors. The numbers of press reports on the incident have been steadily declining and during the last two months there were just two reports. One of them was from a Chinese official, who has still not given up speculations about finding the plane somewhere and the other was from a person who claims to have received a video from a passenger who had hidden his camera in his body, and it shows an isolated island. We have checked the authenticity of the video and found it to be fake. Besides, we had thoroughly checked each and every passenger and did not find any hidden camera."

"We must give full credit to Harold and his team for a very neat clandestine job," remarked John.

Harold smiled and nodded by way of acknowledgement.

Richard continued, "We have interrogated the computer software engineers, presently interned in Area 51, Nevada. They have agreed to their involvement in the development of illegal software, designed to disrupt our computer and data network and have also revealed the names of the organization supporting the project. They have agreed to work for us in projects given by us. They have signed undertakings to that effect."

"That is good news, but how do you keep their identities secret from the probing eyes of the KGB and Chinese intelligence? I'm sure by now they would have figured out their location," surmised John.

"There's no way they can figure out their presence in Area 51. Firstly, nobody has any clue that they have been brought here. They have been transported from Diego Garcia in a B-52 bomber, which halted only at the American bases. Nobody suspects human cargo in a bomber! They travelled at night and were not allowed to get outside the plane. Nobody has seen them. Secondly, their initial landing in Diego Garcia is also unknown to everyone. Now, the only clue, the Boeing 777 plane, has also vanished. Thus, there is no evidence to support their belief that they are in USA. Lastly, no press release or articles have speculated their presence here. This means that no one has ever thought in that direction."

"Your logic seems to be correct, provided they have no access to the outside world through the mobile telephone or other devices. The KGB must have focused their antenna on our air space to catch the faintest signal indicating their presence," said John.

"We have ensured that they do not communicate with the outside world, by fixing "jammers" in their living and working quarters. So, no signal can either be sent or received. The only way of communicating with the outside world is through a central hub, which is out of their bounds," assured Richard."

Della entered the conference room with an urgent message for Richard. He opened the file and said, "Here are some important press releases from Russian newspapers."

"On Wednesday there was a major power blackout in Moscow, which the 'Gazeta' called the biggest energy emergency in Russia's history. It caused panic in parts of Moscow because the Metro stopped without warning, the trolleybuses and trams ground to a halt and televisions and the internet died. It was practically impossible to phone anyone to find out what has happened. The mobile phone services were overloaded and jammed. Several papers dubbed it the end of the world."

"Among the services hit were several hospitals. The most terrifying thing was that the resuscitation systems switched off. The lights went out during operations and the doctors had to use battery-powered torches. One of the paper's reporters saw scenes of panic-buying outside a metro station, as people were unsure whether the power failure was a terrorist attack. For some reason everybody piled into the nearby shops and some started feverishly buying groceries. Some Muscovites, like the taxi drivers, kept a cool head and immediately hiked up the fares after the metro stopped running."

"Inside the metro stations, suddenly the lights went out. People started to walk down the escalators. A huge number of people gathered on the platforms, everybody standing in darkness. There were about five to six policemen and several controllers, but they offered no explanations. The chief of the national grid was earlier quoted as saying that such large-scale power cuts can never happen in Russia."

After reading the file, Richard commented, "This could have been the condition in any of our big cities, or the whole of north USA.""But, we just missed it by a whisker," he added with a smile.

John intervened, "You mean these were done through a computer program!"

"The electric power to Moscow is supplied through two independent feeders from the city substations. In case of failure, data center automatically switches to uninterruptible power supply from 8 Hitec Power Protection Diesel Rotary Devices (DRUPS), with a power output of 1680 kVA each. What happens if a command is given to the data center computer not to switch to DRUPS?" Asked Richard, half in jest.

"Oh! Now I get it! You mean the software that was being developed for use in our country has now been used there?" asked John in amazement.

Richard kept silent and smiled.

Harold took over and said, "The Russian software engineer, Dr. Obukhov, wanted to test the software he developed, on a power system. I advised him to test it on the system in his own country, with which he is quite familiar. He wanted some supplementary data which was available with a particular person he named, but, he added that he would not give the data as it is confidential. I engaged the services of our operator in Moscow, who coaxed him to part with the data on the lure of money. I gave the data to Dr. Obukhov who tried it with the Moscow power system. The first two attempts failed, but the third one apparently succeeded."

John exclaimed, "Now that Russian will know that Dr. Obukhov is here, because he only will need that data for the application of the software."

"No chance! That data is required for many applications and our operator did not tell him the true purpose for which it is required. Besides, on the day of the blackout he had a fatal accident and is not in a position to say anything."

"Great job by everyone!"Remarked John, enthusiastically. "Now, what about the other passengers who were in Flight TG-101?"

Now it was Harold's turn to smile and keep quiet.

"They are being brainwashed and medically treated by our team of doctors. It is too dangerous for them to be released at this point of time. They might divulge everything. After our psychiatrists give us a proper report, we might think of rehabilitating them under new identities somewhere. Most of them have useful qualifications," said Richard.

"I have enough points to brief the President for his July 4 Independence Day address to the nation," said John and dispersed the meeting

Chapter 14

It was a hot July evening in Washington and Richard went for a stroll along the bank of Potomac River to catch a whiff of fresh air. He stood against the railing on the bridge watching the boats sailing down the river. A local policeman with a dog, a German shepherd, passed him, up and down, a couple of times. At one point he stood behind him and said, "Excuse me, Sir, are you having any problem which I can help you solve?"

Richard was confused at the question and asked, "Sorry, what exactly do you want to say?"

The policeman explained, "I have been watching you stand there alone for some time, with a blank stare and a forlorn look on your face, as if contemplating to do something you ought not to do. I thought I might be able to help you desist from doing it, if you confide in me your problem."

Hearing this, Richard had a hearty laugh and said, "No! Nothing of the sort you are thinking! I am also a policeman of a different kind, perhaps. I work in the CIA and I was just spending a little leisure time alone after a grueling fortnight in the office. We are mentally tough, you know, and not prone to doing things you are contemplating."

"I am extremely sorry, Sir," he apologized, while extending his hand towards him. "A few days ago, about this time, a young Chinese lad was standing here in the same way as you are, as I passed him. He was holding a black handbag in his right hand. I was on patrol duty. When I returned, he was nowhere to be seen and the handbag was on the footpath. At first I thought it might be a bomb planted by some terrorist. So I phoned the bomb experts to come and see. They examined the contents of the bag and found nothing resembling a bomb. It only contained some papers, written in Chinese and a floppy disc. I asked some people here if they had seen anyone with a bag. One of them said he saw a Chinese lad going down to the river and he presumed he committed suicide by drowning."

Richard's curiosity was aroused by the story. "Do you have with you the contents of the bag?" he asked.

"Sure, I kept them with me. I can show it to you in my office," he replied.

Richard followed him to his office and took charge of the bag and its contents. He showed him his identity card and said that the bag contained some incriminating materials, which his office would be interested to examine.

Next day he took the bag to his office and gave it to Della and asked her to examine it carefully. She read the manuscripts written in Chinese and said they were instructions for some program which is contained in the floppy disc. Richard felt an urgent need to seek the help of Aiguo in understanding what the program is about. He flew to Nevada the next day and showed the contents of the bag to him.

After examining the contents of the floppy disc, Aiguo said that the program was similar to the one written by him for entering data and computer networks and give commands to the operating system, superimposing the earlier commands. He said that it was most probably written by a computer engineer named Chaoxiang, who was earlier working in his group, but later removed.

"Why was he found with this program in Washington D.C. and why did he leave the bag and go away?" asked Richard.

Aiguo had no definite answer, but said, "Probably after the disappearance of the plane with the Chinese software engineers working in this project, who were presumed dead, he thought of taking it up."

"But why did he come to Washington with it? He could have tested it from there, like you were doing," asked Richard.

"He was probably unable to get grants from the Chinese Academy of sciences for this project and had come looking for a sponsor."

"In that case, why did he leave the bag and go away."

Aiguo thought deeply for a while and came up with a solution.

"As I knew Chaoxiang, he was very ambitious and fond of money. He had probably come to Washington to sell this program to someone. It might have been arranged that he would keep the bag there and the other person would collect it. But, for some inexplicable reason, the other man panicked."

"This makes some sense," opined Richard. "It now remains to be seen who was that person who wanted to buy it and for what purpose?"

Aiguo added, "The program, as such, is not complete and cannot be applied. But, he can complete it after some time and then it can become applicable."

"So we have to find out both these persons, before they are in a position to apply the program. Can you give us some clue to track them?"

Aiguo took his laptop and said, "There was a group photo taken when he was in our group. I'll see if I can find that photo in my laptop."

Aiguo browsed through all the sites where he saved his photos and came up with one photo where he was present.

"Here is the group photo and he is standing in the second row, third from the right."

Richard studied it for some time and requested Aiguo to separate his photo from the others and magnify it, which he did. Richard took a print of the photo and kept it in his briefcase.

"Can you give us any clue about who the other person could be? Obviously, he is also Chinese and could have contacts with some terrorist group. We must try to locate him before it is too late."

"It is difficult to identify him. There are many Chinese who have links with the underworld and terrorist groups," said Aiguo.

Richard returned to CIA headquarters and distributed the photo amongst all intelligence agencies, with a directive to give top priority in locating the person.

After four days, a message was received in his office that a person fitting his photo description was located in Baltimore, close to the CIA headquarters. He was aghast! It was like the bold fly who decided to dine from the mouth of a lion. That person had thrown a challenge that he can do whatever he wants right under the nose of the CIA and he can still evade getting caught. Richard immediately sent out orders that he should be kept under a 24-hour vigil and his tenement searched in his absence to find any incriminating document.

After two days, it was reported that he had not been seen during the last two days and a search of his tenement did not yield any incriminating document. Among the items found were a broken floppy disc, some Chinese literature and a number of Michael Jackson audio discs. Enquiries from his neighbors revealed that he did not socialize with anyone and rarely visited his tenement.

"Back to square one!" exclaimed Richard to himself. He was becoming increasingly impatient with the audacity of that lad and was determined to nail him somehow. He sent his photo to all the international airports, requesting information if he had landed in that airport within the last fifteen days. A day later a message arrived that a man with that photo description had landed in New Jersey airport five days earlier, but his name did not match. He had come by a British Airways flight from London. Enquiries from the immigration authorities yielded a fake address. Very clever indeed, thought Richard! He was now having second thoughts about the purpose of Chaoxiang's visit to USA. Is the Chinese Secret Service having a suspicion that Aiguo is in USA, after the power breakdown in Russia? Has the secret service employed him to search him out?

Chapter 15

Richard decided to pay another visit to Nevada and meet Aiguo. He posed this problem to him and asked, "Is it possible for the Russian authorities to track down the source of the command that caused the recent power breakdown?"

"No, it's not possible. The command is sent in an encrypted form through their data network and designed only to prevent the computer from following the command that is already saved in the system. It cannot be traced," he replied.

"Is there any reason to believe that the Chinese Secret Service or the KGB has a suspicion about your involvement in this power breakdown?"

"I doubt it! Of course, they know that we were developing a software for a similar purpose against the USA, but, unless they have a reason to believe that we are alive, they can't have any suspicion. Perhaps, you know better if they still have the notion that our Flight had crashed and we are all 'dead'!"

"So far, we have no contrary information about their belief that the plane had crashed. But, they must surely be wondering why there has been no debris found yet. That might motivate them to initiate a search."

"Where is the plane, anyway," asked Aiguo.

"Sorry! I can't answer that. It's a state secret, you know. It will be better if you also do not know the answer!" he replied.

"I know! Honestly, I'm not much bothered about the plane. I'm worried about my work, my family here and in China. Nothing should happen to them."

"Nothing will happen to them if you don't do anything indiscreet, like trying to contact them. In that case it will set the cat among the pigeon and may destroy everyone, including your family. We will try to bring to you up-to-date information about your family in China, from time to time, through our operators based in China. If you want to send anything to them, it can be arranged incognito, provided you don't disclose who the sender is. After a few years, everything will be forgotten and you can go back to China, or lead a very prosperous life as a free citizen in this country. The choice is yours!"

"I am happy working here and have made many friends, but, sometimes I just remember them."

"Yes, that is natural. I'm sure you'll soon overcome your sentiments and love the working environment here. I wanted to ask you if you know something more about your friend, Chaoxiang. Currently, he is hiding somewhere and we have no idea about his whereabouts. The longer it takes to track him, the more difficult it will become to prevent him from carrying out his plans. We also do not know what his plans are? You say that the program that he has brought is not complete and cannot be applied to inflict any damage like the recent Russian disaster. Then, could it be that his target is to search you?"

"Me?! !" asked Aiguo in a panicked tone.

"Don't be panicky! This is just a speculation. You have nothing to fear as long as you are here under our protection. His planting the bag containing the program and instructions in Chinese in a conspicuous place, not very far from the CIA headquarters and then performing the disappearing act has set me thinking. If there is a suspicion that the CIA is behind the disappearance of Flight 101, this is bait for you to respond, which will verify if the suspicion is true or false."

"How do they expect me to respond?"

"Since he had been you colleague, the normal response is to try and contact him by some way. You may apply the software which you have developed on some American city, which will prove that you are alive and in CIA custody. He will then search you out."

"Doesn't the power breakdown in Russia prove that I'm alive?"

"They are not very sure about that. It could possibly be developed secretly by the American software engineers and applied on Russia about which they may not be aware!"

"If I don't respond at all, it means I am dead!" asked Aiguo.

"In the present scenario, yes! But, I would suggest that you also set up bait to draw him out of his hiding place, so that we know his true purpose. In CIA we sometimes get a situation where an operator has defected to the opposite camp. We have to get him back fast before he does major damage. We set up bait to get him back by asking his wife, or girlfriend, to send a coded message asking him to return home early due to mother's illness. This works many times. Can you think of something similar?"

Aiguo thought for a while and said, "My elder sister, who is an expert on Oriental arts and is an art teacher in Lanzhou, knew Chaoxiang's family well. He is very close to his mother. She used to live with him in Lanzhou. I don't know her present whereabouts. How is it possible to set up bait?"

"Do you know some weakness in him that can be exploited? For example, does he have a fondness for beautiful, sexy women? We found lots of Chinese literature in the tenement he was staying. What kind of literature does he read? Is he a big fan of Michael Jackson, as we found MJ discs, too?"

Aiguo tried hard to recollect his past associations with him. "Once I had gone to his room where he was staying and saw several nude photos of Chinese and Hollywood actresses on the wall besides his bed. He also used to imitate Michael Jackson and dance like him, sometimes. I don't know much about his reading habits."

Richard made notes of what he heard and asked a final question. "Do you know if he had some friends or relatives, living in USA?"

"I had heard he had a cousin brother living in Chinatown, somewhere in the west coast of USA."

Richard bid him good-bye and went back to CIA headquarters with a new plan of action.

***

He called his operators and told them to search the Chianatown area of Baltimore thoroughly and inquire about Chaoxiang in some Chinese–run laundry, or hotel. He forbade them on showing his photo. "If someone turns up and identifies himself as Chaoxiang, tell him that a friend of his wants to meet him. Give him the address of our safe house in Baltimore, where our security staff will be waiting in plain clothes at the appointed time," he said.

Next day an operator named Sam rang up and said, "There is no Chinatown, as such, only a block of about 300 tenements at Park Avenue, between Saratoga and Mulberry. I scouted the area and asked for Chaoxiang at many places, with negative results. In one restaurant named China Doll, a person claimed he knows somebody by that name. I asked him some details about his residence in China and date of his visit, which tallied with the information available with me. I then asked him if he could convey a message to him. He agreed. I told him that my lady friend wishes to meet him on a matter of great importance and would be waiting for him at the given address at 4 p.m. tomorrow."

Richard gave Della this information and told him about his plan.

"You are to dress in your seductive best and put as much Chinese make-up as possible. You will reach that address before the time of appointment and wait. I will also be there. In all probability, Chaoxiang will not come and somebody else, using his identity, will come. We have to believe that he is Chaoxiang and treat him as such. You have to tell him a story. You were in the plane that crashed into the sea, sitting next to Aiguo. You were the sole survivor, because luckily, you were thrown away from the falling plane, dressed in your inflatable life-vest. This prevented you from being drawn into the draft created by the sinking plane."

"You became unconscious and kept floating in the sea. You were picked up by a fishing trawler and taken to a port, where you were admitted in a local hospital. Next day, you were air-lifted to a big hospital in the town, whose name you do not recollect. After a few days' stay, you were flown to USA by the American embassy officials, to your hometown, Washington. You were admitted to a hospital, where you recovered fully. Your purse had always been with you and when you opened it one day, you found the name, address and phone number of Li Na, elder sister of Aiguo, who lived in Lanzhou. You contacted her to pay your condolences and to return a very special article worn by him, which had come in your possession by accident. She told you that a person by the name of Chaoxiang, who worked in the same Research Center, had gone to Baltimore and she could contact him. That is why you wanted to meet him. Then you make up another story of how you met Aiguo in Bangkok. But remember; say everything very confidently and with a little acting to make your story look realistic!"

Della listened to 'her' story attentively and asked, "Am I allowed slight modification of the story, if the situation demands? Of course! The Bangkok story I can make up convincingly."

"By all means! Only ensure that the proper links are maintained so that he does not suspect," replied Richard.

The next day Della got dressed in a tight-fitting, navy-blue colored miniskirt, with afrilled plunging neckline, deep enough to make the cleavage visible. A matching Chinese hair-do made her look at her seductive best. She reached the address of the meeting well before the appointed time and waited patiently in the sitting room. Security men dressed in plain clothes were positioned around the building and on the road away from the house. Richard entered the building through a side entrance and positioned himself in the adjacent room, behind the curtain, so that he could get a clear glimpse of Della and the person sitting in the chair in front her.

Soon after 4 p.m. a Chinese man was seen lumbering towards the house, stopping at intervals to check the address.

Richard saw him and knew that he was not Chaoxiang. He signaled Della to be ready to receive him. He entered the house and pressed the calling bell. Della herself got up and opened the door with a smile.

"I am Chaoxiang living in Chinatown. I was given this address and told that someone wanted to see me on a matter of great importance," he said, by way of introduction.

Della nodded and said, "Yes, I sent my friend to search you and request you to come here to meet me. I am Margaret Morris. Please come in and be seated. I am thankful to you for sparing some time to come here and meet me."

He appeared to be very impressed with Della and kept feasting his eyes on her physical attributes as he slowly walked towards the chair.

"Actually, I am not Chaoxiang, but his cousin brother. Chao came here only four days ago and is not well today. I came in his place to receive the important message and I will convey it to him," he said apologetically.

"Doesn't matter!" cooed Della. "When is your brother returning to China?"

"He is returning next week and may extend the stay by a few days if his work is not done."

"Has he come here for work? I thought he is on a holiday," asked Della.

"He is on a holiday, but he has some personal work which he wants to complete."

"The purpose for which I wanted to meet him is too tragic to explain in words," Della began on a solemn note in Chinese. "I met Aiguo and his wife in Bangkok, while we were staying in the same hotel. I am a lover of Oriental art and paintings and had gone to Bangkok as a tourist. We spent lot of time together and visited the art museums, temples and other places of interest together. Aiguo and his wife were busy with the lectures in an Institute and so we planned the visits during their free times. On the day of their departure for London he came to my room, along with Chunhua, to show me a special oriental charm in the form of a locket, attached to a golden chain. It was given to him by a Chinese holy man, or Xian, to protect him from all evil. They left for a farewell dinner, leaving the charm with me and said they would collect it on their return. Before leaving, Aiguo had given her the name, address and telephone number of his elder sister who resided in Lanzhou. She was also a great lover of Oriental arts and had a good collection of paintings and sculptures. Aiguo had told her to visit his sister in China for knowing more about Oriental arts."

"I had kept the address and the charm in an inner pocket of my purse and forgot all about it. The Aiguos came late at night and left for the airport to catch their flight to London. Next morning I heard about the disappearance of their plane, believed to have crashed into the sea. I was too shocked to believe it. I returned home and hoped to hear that Aiguo and his wife are alive, but it was not to be. After many days, I accidentally opened that pocket in my purse where the charm and the address of his sister were kept. I thought I must return it to its rightful owner. I phoned his sister to pay my condolences and told her everything. She suggested that I should deliver it to Chaoxiang, who worked in the same Center as Aiguo and was now in Baltimore. She said she would collect it from him, when he returns. This is the purpose of meeting Chaoxiang,"

Della shed a few crocodile tears to increase the solemnity of the occasion and waited for his reaction. He stood up and said, "It's indeed a very tragic event. I shall bring Chaoxiang in an hour and he will deliver the charm to Aiguo's sister."

After his departure Richard told the secret service men to tail him and carry out plan 2. He then turned to Della and clapped, "Your performance has been excellent and your story was much more convincing than the one suggested by me. No hospitalization, no floating dangerously in water! The way you acted made me wonder why you were not in Hollywood!"

"Thank you for paying me such high compliments! It's talking in Chinese that did the trick! He simply got carried away."

"Perhaps, your Chinese might have had a little effect, but I suppose, your seductive look was the most important factor that completely disarmed him. You must remember, Chaoxiang has an eye for beautiful women and had their nude photos pasted on the wall of his bedroom. I am expecting him to arrive here before one hour!"

Della smiled and said, "Now, I understand why you asked me to be in my seductive best!"

Richard grinned mischievously and walked to the exit to await their arrival.

Chapter 16

Chaoxiang's brother left in his car, after his meeting with Della, closely followed by the secret service men in their car. He went to Park Avenue and stopped in front of an old building. He went inside and was met by several men, with whom he was having a discussion. Meanwhile, plan 2 was being executed by the secret service men. They opened the boot space in his car and closed it after keeping a few packets of heroin. They went back and sat in their car and phoned the National Drug Law Enforcement Agency (NDLEA),informing them the car details.

Chaoxiang and his brother left in the car after 15 minutes, oblivious of the packages in the boot. On the way the NDLEA officials intercepted them and demanded an inspection of the car. They had brought sniffer dogs with them who sniffed the inside of the car. They closed in on the boot and gave indication of something. The officials asked them to open the boot and the heroin packets were found neatly concealed in a leather bag kept in the corner. The occupants of the car were immediately arrested and charged with the possession of banned substances, despite their protests. They were put in a lockup, pending investigation.

Next day a lawyer working for the CIA approached the concerned authorities and submitted a petition on behalf of the arrested persons, seeking release on bail. He had brought the necessary deposit and signed papers for their release. The two brothers were whisked away in a car to an unknown location and kept in separate rooms, under tight security. Richard entered the room of Chaoxiang and introduced himself as a friend, who wishes to help him get back to his country as early as possible.

"Your charges are serious and under USA laws you might get sentenced to 99 years in prison. This means you will never be able to get out of prison. This is rather harsh on a young, promising man like you, with such good education," he told him.

"I have been framed. I did not carry any banned substance," he shouted agitatedly.

"But, it was found in the car in which you were travelling. The car was registered in the name of your brother. How would you deny the charge?"

"Anybody can put it in my car in my absence. How can I be charged for possession of this substance?"

"Of course! That is a possibility! But, again you have to prove that someone else did put it in the boot of your car without your knowledge."

Chaoxiang was confused. "How can I prove that? I was not in the car at that moment."

"The DA will not accept your denial. He will insist you are just trying to mislead the court."

"Then what should I do?" he said in a mood of abject surrender.

"You must share with me some details and take me into your confidence," suggested Richard.

"Firstly, what is your qualification and your profession?"

"I am a computer software engineer and I work at the Telecommunication Research Center in Lanzhou, China."

"When did you arrive in USA and for what purpose?"

"I arrived in USA four days ago, just to meet my brother."

"When did you last meet your brother?"

"I met him many years ago when I was still in college."

"What was the urgent need to meet him again after so many years?"

Chaoxiang thought for a while before answering, "He was having serious medical problems and so I wanted to meet him. My mother was also keen to know his exact condition."

"What was his medical problem?"

"He had liver problems and acute diabetes."

Richard decided to check these statements with his brother, who was in an adjacent room. He took leave of Chaoxiang for a couple of minutes. On the way out, he told the secret service personnel to bring the bag which was collected from the police and was in the boot of his car.

***

His brother was being interrogated by another officer from the CIA. Richard entered the room and greeted him, before seating himself.

"How is your diabetes?" was his first question.

He looked puzzled and repeated, "Diabetes?" "I have no diabetes."

Richard said, "Your brother said you're suffering from acute diabetes."

"Oh, no! I had a little problem with the kidney some time ago, but now it is OK."

"Is he your real brother? How much younger is he compared to your age?"

"We are first cousins and I am about eight years older than him," he replied.

"Are you working in USA and for how long?"

"My father-in-law used to run a hotel in Chinatown here. He had called us to help him. So we came here ten years ago. He died four years ago. Now I run the hotel."

"Did you go back to China after coming here?"

"No!"

"Why did your brother come here?"

He scratched his head and smiled. "He sent me mail that he has got some urgent work here. I told him to stay with me and I will take him wherever he wants to go."

"Which places did you take him to visit and which places did he visit on his own?"

"I took him to Washington for sight-seeing one day and next day he went on his own."

"Did he plan to visit some other places?"

"He said he was going to go to Philadelphia tomorrow, but now it seems impossible."

"Have you any idea about what was his urgent work?"

"No! I suppose it has something to do with the computer. He was always doing something with his laptop."

"Has your brother met any other person during his stay?"

"The only persons he met are my friends. I have not seen him meet anybody else."

Richard then showed him the bag and asked, "Did you see this bag in the possession of your brother anytime?"

He looked at it closely and answered, "I have not seen him with this bag."

"Does any friend of his, resides alone close to your hotel."

"I have not seen him meeting any of his friends. But, on the second day, after dinner, he went for a walk and returned quite late. When I asked him, he said that he had gone on a very long walk."

"Thank you! I'll try to do my best to get you both released early. I have to take your leave now."

***

Richard went back to Chaoxiang and said, "I'm disappointed! You've lied to me."

Chaoxiang was startled. "I have not lied. I told you the truth!"

"I asked your brother and he says he does not have diabetes."

"He keeps thinking he doesn't have diabetes. But, he has acute diabetes. His wife told my mother on phone."

"Who is his doctor? Why will he imagine he doesn't have diabetes when he has it?"

"I don't know the name of his doctor, but I have seen him injecting himself many times."

"OK! Now, tell me, which was your port of entry in USA and the name of the airlines?"

"I disembarked in New Jersey and came by British Airways flight from London."

"Why did you come via London, when there are direct flights from China to USA?"

"I wanted to discuss with a consultant about my project."

"What is your project and who was this consultant?"

"I am working on a project concerning the design of data networks in telecommunications. I can't tell you the name of the consultant."

"Can't or won't? I believe he was not your consultant at all!"

Chaoxiang kept quiet and turned his head.

"Your silence tells me my belief is correct. You are lying again. If you want us to help you must speak the truth. You have not met anyone connected with your stated official project."

"I am not lying!" he said angrily.

"Then tell me who was it that you met in London and in what connection? Was it a drug peddler?"

"No! I've already told you that I don't take drugs and don't deal with it."

"How's it then that heroin was found in the car in which you were travelling?"

"I told you it was planted."

"By whom? Does your brother take drugs, or is he a drug peddler?"

"No!"

"Where was he taking you when you were apprehended by the officials from NDLEA?"

"He was taking me to a lady who said she wanted to send some parcel to a friend in China, whom I know."

"Do you know this lady and who is your friend to whom she was sending the parcel?"

"I don't know this lady. A friend of hers met my brother in his hotel and said she wanted to meet me. My brother met her and she told him that she wanted to send something to my friend in Lanzhou."

"Does your friend also work in the same office as yourself?"

"Actually, she is the elder sister of my former colleague, who died tragically recently in a plane crash. She is our family friend and this lady wanted to send her a parcel."

"Sorry to hear about your colleague! What was his name and how did it happen?"

"His name was Aiguo and he was working on an important project. He was going from Bangkok to London and the plane disappeared without a trace. It was believed to have crashed."

"Yes, I've read about it and seen the TV coverage. How is it possible that the entire plane disappeared without a trace? Was it the work of a terrorist organization?"

"Nothing is known yet. Nobody has claimed responsibility for the disappearance."

"You said your friend was working on an important project. Has it got anything to do with the disappearance?"

Chaoxiang thought for a while and answered, "They could have kidnapped him, instead of making the entire plane disappear."

"What was so important in that project which attracted their attention? Do you have any idea?"

"I heard he was working on designing software for controlling the power supply system in any country."

"It means that if a terrorist organization gets hold of this software it can blackmail the government of that country, by threatening to turn their power supply off! Has Aiguo completed the project work?"

"It was a top secret project and I do not know the details. It is rumored that he sold the software to somebody, but there is no evidence."

"He must have got a very big sum of money for it. How is the disappearance of the plane linked to it?"

"It's a complex problem. I can't think of it. Maybe, the plane has not actually disappeared, but hidden somewhere. Possibly, Aiguo and the others are also alive. These are all speculations!"

"Speculations are based on some facts. It is said that there can be no smoke without fire. If you see the smoke, then there must be fire somewhere. Are there some hidden facts which you don't want to share, or afraid to share? You are already embroiled in a drug case for which you can get a very long sentence. If you can present facts that can help me turn around the case to a different angle, it is possible your sentence may be reduced considerably!"

After a delay of several minutes, he said, "Two days after the supposed disappearance of the plane, someone in the Center heard a faint voice in his i-phone saying that they are all alive and well and the plane had not crashed. After that the voice suddenly became inaudible. He and some other colleagues tried to reconnect with that number, but it was switched off. Then we tried to trace the call, without success. Apparently, the call was bounced off several servers before being received here. We could guess it was from somewhere in the western hemisphere, from the date, which was one day behind our date."

"That is a very important observation. Did you share it with everyone?"

"No, we kept it strictly among ourselves, for fear it may endanger the lives of the survivors if the kidnappers came to know about it."

"Very intelligent thinking," opined Richard. "You should keep it strictly confidential till further evidence is found. Any other observation?"

"I can't think of any at the moment."

"Was the purpose of your visit to London and USA connected to locating the source of that message?"

"No! By now they might have destroyed the SIM cards of the phone and, so, it is impossible to locate the source."

"You must tell me a viable purpose of your visit here, which I can present to the court. Otherwise, the DA will press the charge of drug peddling as the sole purpose of your visit. You help me, in order that I help you."

"I came to see my brother, who is seriously ill"

"That is a lie. The DA will easily prove it and add the charge of perjury to that of drug peddling."

Richard then showed him the bag and said, "This is your last chance to come out with the truth. Can you identify this bag?"

Chaoxiang looked at and said, "I have never seen it."

"Again you're lying! How am I going to convince you about the importance of speaking the truth, for your own sake," said Richard angrily. "OK, here are the contents of the bag. Do you not recognize your own handwriting in Chinese? Here's your floppy disc."

He looked at the contents and said, "These items don't belong to me."

Richard angrily snatched the bag, along with its contents, from Chaoxiang and walked out saying, "I don't think I can help you. You're consistently lying. You will be dropped at your place and face the ordeal when the case comes up for hearing."

He ordered that both the brothers be dropped at their residence. He told the secret police to keep a close watch on their movements and report to him.

Chapter 17

Richard returned to his office at the CIA headquarters, crestfallen, at having failed to get the truth from Chaoxiang. Della tried her best to console him, “He will breakdown sooner or later. We have to keep on trying. He seems to be a hard nut to crack.”

“You know, Della, this guy is a habitual liar. He continues to lie, despite my telling him bluntly that he is lying. The bag belongs to him, the instructions have been handwritten by him, the floppy disc is loaded by him and yet, he goes on denying it. Aiguo has identified the handwriting as his and I personally, believe him,” he lamented.

“Perhaps, he is a keen student of German history during the regime of Hitler. His deputy, Joseph Goebbels, the propaganda chief had coined the famous saying, ’if you keep telling lies repeatedly, it becomes truth.’ I admire his tenacity,” said Della, in a lighter vein.

“OK, I’ll give you an opportunity to admire him more closely. You’ll have to go once again to that house and use all your charm, to extract the required information.”

She accepted the challenge with a smile and said, “My pleasure!”

“You have to phone the hotel, ‘China Doll’ and ask for Chaoxiang. Most probably, his brother will take your call. Ask him why his brother had not come to see you, as he had assured. He will give some excuses. Ask him to bring his brother today evening, if possible. Hear his reply and report to me.”

Della did as told. Sure enough, Chaoxiang's brother took the call.

Della spoke in her sweetest voice, "Hello, I was waiting for you to return with your brother, but you did not come."

"We were coming when we met with a small accident and had to report to the police station. We are all right now and shall try to come today evening. We're sorry that we could not come yesterday," he said.

"Oh my God! I hope you were not hurt! Will it be possible for you to come today at 4 p.m.?" Della asked.

"Yes, today we shall definitely come," he asserted.

Della reported the conversation to Richard and they made preparations to go to that house once again. Meanwhile, a message was received by Richard that Chaoxiang had gone out alone to a departmental store where he met another Chinese man. He had a conversation with that man for around 15 minutes, after which he returned. The secret service men made discreet enquiries about him and found he worked in the shoe stall, as an assistant. His name is Huang Fu and he lived alone in a tenement nearby. Richard called a Chinese operator working in the CIA and told him to visit the shoe stall in that departmental store and establish friendship with him, to collect more information about him.

Della reached the house well before 4 p.m. and waited once again, dressed in her customized apparel used on such occasions. Richard and his team of secret service men were positioned nearby. It was past 4 p.m. and there was no trace of the expected visitors. At that moment a message was received by Richard that they have started and are on their way.

Chaoxiang followed his brother into the house and was introduced to Della. She welcomed him in the most elegant manner, allowing a gentle smile to escape her thin lips and extending the tip of her fingers to be touched by his hand. She invited him to be seated. His brother left after the introduction, on the pretext of some urgent work. Chaoxiang was overawed by her physical presence and kept ogling at her as much as he could.

"I hope you have not been hurt by the accident," she asked with an expression of concern.

"No, it was not an accident. Somebody planted some banned substances in the boot of our car in our absence and informed the drug agency. They stopped our car and after searching it booked us for possession of banned substances."

"Oh, my God! How terrible! Who could have done this? Do you have an enemy here who is out to harass you?"

"Enemy? I came only ten days ago. How can I have enemies?"

"Do you have any friends, other than your brother, of course!"

"Yes, I have a few friends, but I don't know them well enough."

"I know some important people in the agency who can help you. If you bring your friends to me I shall tell them what to do. Your problem will be solved," she said with an air of authority.

"You are also my friend, I hope," he said in anticipation of an affirmative answer.

"Yes, of course! But, there are certain things which I cannot do on my own. I require somebody's help."

"I'll ask them if they are willing to help."

"If they are your friend, they'll certainly help. If you bring them to me I shall persuade them to help you," she said with a smile.

"What is it that you wish to send to your friend in China?" he asked, for want of anything else to talk about.

"What's the hurry?" she asked with a smile. "Would you like to have some drinks? Red wine!"

He hesitated a moment before saying, "I don't mind it!"

Della poured wine in two glasses and offered one to him.

"I'm fortunate that you came here from Lanzhou, so I could send the parcel to its rightful owner. Did you come on official work?" she said.

"You can say it's official!" he said with an air of diffidence.

"Aiguo used to tell me that he was working on the development of software for network applications. Are you also working in the same project?"

"I was working in the same project, but was later given another project."

"Aiguo said he was having a friend in USA, with whom he was in frequent correspondence and occasionally contacted him in London. But, he never told me his name or address. Do you know him?"

"I don't know his friend and never contacted him."

Della poured some more wine in his glass and sat closer to him on the sofa.

"Who is your friend here? Is he of Chinese origin or American?"

"He is of Chinese origin, but has been staying here for many years. He works in a shoe shop. His name is Huang Fu."

"How did you know him? Is it through some Chinese relative living in China?"

"His brother works in our Center in Lanzhou. He told me that some people in USA are interested in our project and would like to discuss with me. He told me to meet him in USA."

"You must be careful while meeting strangers here. How long have you known Huang Fu?"

"I came to know him after I came here. He appears to be a decent person."

"Everybody appears decent when you meet him for the first time. Does he stay close to your brother's place?"

"He has a tenement there, but he does not stay there most of the time. He shares an apartment with his girlfriend somewhere else."

"Such people can be dangerous. You don't know anything about him, or the kind of people he is associated with. You had said that somebody had planted drug packets in your car, in your absence. It is possible that somebody associated with him has done it! Has he told you that he would take you to meet someone?"

"He had told me that he would take me to Philadelphia to meet someone who is interested in my project."

"Has he told you his name and have you given him any documents, like computer programs, floppy discs, etc., that explains the work that you are doing?"

Della again poured a little wine into his glass to help him reveal the truth.

"He once asked me to explain the work that I am doing. So I explained to him on a piece of paper the work I am doing which was contained in the floppy. He told me he would talk with the other person before taking me to meet him."

"Do you know what has happened to that paper and floppy?"

"He took it from me and kept it with himself."

"When did you show him your work and when was the last time you met him?"

"I met him the day after I came here, to explain my work and the last time was today morning."

"When did he say he would take you to Philadelphia?"

"He said tomorrow afternoon and indicated I may have to stay there for another day."

"I am concerned about you. You have not told me the name of the other person; otherwise I could have verified his reputation through my sources. Anyway, I have an idea. The parcel which I am sending to my friend's sister is a charm, attached to a chain, which is supposed to protect the wearer from any harm. It protected me from death. I was to fly by the same flight as Aiguo, but had to cancel the flight at the last moment owing to my indisposition. I request you wear it and, I'm sure, it will protect you from any harm. You must meet me after your return from Philadelphia and tell me everything that had happened."

Della got up and gave the necklace to him, urging him to wear it immediately. Chaoxiang did as he was told and bid her good-night before departing from the house.

Richard was pleased with the way the meeting went and complimented Della for her stellar performance.

"Now we can easily hear all the conversations, between Chaoxiang and others, because the charm is actually a mini transmitter and transmits the conversations to a nearby earphone receiver, worn by the secret service man following him. It also contains a mini recorder to record the conversations."

"What if he takes the charm to China and gives it to Aiguo's sister?" asked Della looking concerned.

"Don't worry, he will not be allowed to leave the shores of USA, at least, in the near future."

***

A message reached Richard from his operator that Huang Fu also worked in a gambling den cum bar, in downtown Baltimore. His girlfriend worked as a striptease dancer and he spent most of his time in her company. This den was frequented by many well-known Mafia dons and Huang Fu was known to have contacts with some of them.

Richard ordered the reinforcement of the secret service men and continuous surveillance on Chaoxiang and Huang Fu. In the morning a message came that the two had met after dinner for a short time in Huang Fu's tenement. Chaoxiang asked him about the floppy disc and the handwritten explanations. He said it had been sent to the concerned person whom they are going to meet. They are leaving for Philadelphia in the afternoon in his car.

Richard and Della sat in their office discussing the case. "The ownership of the bag, which contained the papers and the floppy, is still a mystery. Apparently, it did not belong to Chaoxiang, because he never talked about it. Then it must belong to someone else who kept the floppy and papers in it and then left it on the bank of the Potomac. The important question that arises is why did he keep it where it was found and then disappear? Was the act deliberate, or was it forced by something he saw, or was afraid of?"

Della thought for a while and remarked, "From the conversation with me, it appears that Chaoxiang was not aware that his manuscript and floppy were kept on the bank of the Potomac. When he asked Huang Fu about it, he replied that it was given to the person whom he is going to meet. It is likely that either Huang Fu, or somebody else who received the contents from him, has kept it there."

"You're right. But the questions which baffle us are, 'Who' and 'Why'?"

A message was received by Richard that Huang Fu and Chaoxiang have reached Philadelphia and Huang Fu has taken him to a casino, named Sugarhouse Casino, in Delaware avenue. It is known to be frequented by some of the mafia dons, notably George Borgesi and his men.

"We're slowly and steadily moving towards the end of the tunnel," he muttered to himself. A little later another message came that an undercover agent working for the FBI, has been engaged to gain entry into the casino and track them. Initially, they were untraceable, but later they were found to be closeted in a closed cabin, with two other men. One of the men told him to give him the floppy and demonstrate how it works. He promised to give an advance of fifty grand if it works. They came out of the cabin and were shown round the casino by a bar girl. Huang Fu played a few games in which he won and lost in a few others. They returned to the car and are now on their way home.

Richard ordered his men to pick them up for questioning next morning, in the usual CIA guest house.

Huang Fu and Chaoxiang were brought to the interrogation room of the CIA and kept in separate rooms. Richard entered Chaoxiang's room first and said, "Good Morning! We meet again! Although it is futile to ask you anything, because you'll just tell a lie, I have to seek certain answers from you."Richard noticed that he was not wearing the charm, which means his conversations with him won't be transmitted.

Chaoxiang was silent, but from the expression on his face he conveyed that he did not agree with the charge.

Richard reminded him, "You are still under the charge of drug peddling and can be called to appear before the court any time to face trial. This is your last opportunity to try and absolve yourself of these charges. Are you willing to cooperate?"

He nodded in the affirmative.

Richard again showed the bag and its contents and asked, "Is this your bag and floppy and is the handwritten stuff written by you?"

He remained silent for a while and answered, "The bag is not mine, but the floppy and the handwritten papers are mine. Where did you get it?"

"That you have to tell us. Where did you expect it to be found? Did you give it to someone?"

He was in two minds whether to answer or not. Eventually he decided to answer, "My friend Huang Fu told me that some people were interested in my project and I should give my software and how to use it. I gave it to him. Later, when I asked him about it, he said that he has given it to the concerned person. I am seeing it only now."

Richard assured him, “We are not the concerned person your friend Huang Fu referred to. Actually, these stuffs were put in the bag and placed on the bank of the Potomac. It was picked up by a policeman on patrol duty. Can you throw some light as to how it reached that place?”

He looked surprised and said, “I have no idea how it reached that place. Perhaps Huang Fu may know.”

Richard thought it was time to interrogate Huang Fu and went to the adjacent room, after excusing himself.

***

Richard greeted Huang Fu and introduced himself, as he entered his room and said, “Huang, your friend Chaoxiang is in deep trouble and has been booked for possession of banned drugs. He says, and I believe him, that these were planted to harass him. I need to know certain facts which will prove that he is not a drug peddler. Can you help me?”

Huang Fu replied, “I know him only after he came here and met me. I can tell you all that I know since that time.”

“I will ask you about certain facts which happened during that time. The first thing that I want to know is whether Chaoxiang gave you some papers and a floppy disc.”

“He gave me some handwritten papers and a floppy disc related to the project he is doing.”

“Did he tell you why he is giving it to you?”

“He said some people are interested in his project and want to discuss with him.”

“Do you know those people and whether he had any discussion with them?”

“I don’t know. He has not told me anything.”

Richard then took out the bag and its contents and asked, "Do you recognize these items?"

Huang Fu's face turned crimson and said hurriedly, "These belong to Chaoxiang. I don't know anything about it."

"Does this bag also belong to him?"

He stared at it intently for some time and said, "I put those papers and the floppy in it so that they are not misplaced."

"So, this bag belongs to you. It was found on the bank of the Potomac. Can you tell me how it reached there?"

He struggled for an answer and eventually said, "I don't know."

"How can you say you don't know? It is your bag and cannot go there on its own. Either, you have taken it there, or someone else has taken it. Which is correct?"

He kept quiet.

Richard said, "You cannot get away by refusing to speak. You get into deeper trouble by being accused as an accessory in the drug possession case."

"I want to speak to my lawyer."

"At present you have to speak only to me. Your lawyer can come in only after you are formally charged. If you cooperate, both of you can go scot free. Otherwise, we have methods to extract the truth, but it will hurt you. Now, are you willing to state the facts?"

Huang Fu looked around helplessly and discovered that the only way out of this predicament is to state the facts. He asked, "Will I be freed if I state the facts?"

"We will have to cross-check the facts and see if it's true. Only then, we shall decide the next course of action. If you speak the truth, you have nothing to worry."

Huang Fu began, "After I got the floppy disc and papers from Chaoxiang, I put them in my bag and called my friend, Max. He was having contact with the people who were interested in the project. He told me to wait near the bridge on the Potomac River. I was sitting on a bench and saw a newspaper describe the Russian power breakdown on the front page. I heard from Chaoxiang that the program on his floppy can cause similar breakdowns by connecting with the data networks through remote control and transmitting the appropriate commands. Meanwhile, I saw a police patrol going up and down the bank. I thought that if they see me with this floppy they might suspect me of being responsible for it. I got panicky and left the bag in a corner and came home."

"Who is Max and how does he have contact with the people who are interested in this project?"

"I met him in the gambling den cum bar, in downtown Baltimore. My girlfriend, Yeti, works as a dancer. Max has many contacts in the underworld. He was aware of the existence of software that could control the power supply in a city, remotely, bypassing the official channels. When I heard about Chaoxiang's project I contacted Max. He told me that there is a lot of money in this project, if he was willing to share it with some interested people. He told me to take that floppy and give it to him. He would then contact the interested people and fix the price."

"Did you contact those interested people and where?"

"When he failed to turn up, I contacted Max again. He gave me an address in Philadelphia and told me to contact George. I took Chaoxiang to Philadelphia and went to the address, which was a casino. I asked for George and was taken to a cabin. Somebody by the name of George met us. He discussed the project with Chaoxiang, but since he was not having the floppy, he asked him to demonstrate the software and he was willing to pay an advance."

"What excuse did Max give for not turning up?"

"He said he was held up on some urgent work and was unable to contact him."

"Do you believe that Max was telling the truth. Or, is it that he also saw the police patrol and decided to vamoose?"

"They are hardened criminals. I don't think he would be afraid of a police patrol."

"How much advance did George promise to give?"

"Fifty grand!"

"That is a big amount of money. Would your friend not be tempted to sell the product?"

"Yes, he would! He came all the way from China to sell his software and make money."

"Assuming that Chaoxiang's software does succeed in bringing about a power breakdown, why would a gangster be interested in a scientific project like this?"

"The gangsters are interested in using the period of power breakdown, in robbing stores, jewelry shops and banks. They can also blackmail the city administration by threatening to cause a severe disruption in all the services unless they are paid ransom."

"I see! By helping the gangsters in their nefarious activities, both you and your friend become accessories to the crime and liable to be sentenced for a term in prison."

Huang Fu looked meekly at Richard and said, "I have cooperated with you and answered all your questions truthfully, but you are still sending me to prison!"

"I am looking from the legal, as well as the moral point of view. In your quest for money you will put millions of people into inconvenience and cause billions of dollars loss to the nation, of which you are a part. Should you be helping them, or help the nation bring such people to be punished under the legal system?"

Huang Fu was visibly shaken and said nothing.

Richard went back to Chaoxiang to continue the interrogation.

Chapter 18

"The question about how the bag and its contents reached the place where it was found, has been solved. Huang Fu took it there to give it to someone, who did not turn up," Richard told Chaoxiang after he entered his room. "Now you have to tell us about your trip to Philadelphia."

"Huang Fu took me to a casino to meet someone by the name of George. He was interested in my software and said he would buy it if I demonstrate how it works."

"How much did he offer you?"

"He promised an advance of fifty grand if I give him the floppy."

"Are you willing to accept the offer? You must remember that your floppy will be used for destructive purposes that can cause untold damages to the nation. You will be helping them in their criminal activity, in return for a small amount of money. You can be charged of being an accessory to their crimes."

"I have not accepted their offer and given them the floppy."

"You have come all the way from China just to sell your floppy, irrespective of the consequences. Huang Fu was your conduit in this quest for money"

Chaoxiang said nothing.

Richard continued, "Is your software ready for use?"

"I have to do some more work and test it, before it can be used."

"Will you cooperate with us and help us nab those criminals, if we help you to complete the work on your software? You have no choice. If you don't cooperate, we will charge you of trying to wage a war against our nation by helping certain criminals. The punishment can be 99 years in prison!"

Chaoxiang thought for a while and agreed to cooperate.

Richard told him with air of finality, "You will go back to your lodging and pretend not to have discussed anything with me. You will not tell anyone, including your friend, what transpired between us and you will not leave the place under any circumstance. Our men will be constantly watching you. After two days, I will take you to a place where you will work with one of our expert software engineer and complete the software. A test site will be arranged, where you will demonstrate the software in the presence of those men. It will work successfully and they will give you the promised advance, in exchange for the floppy. Your role will end there and we take over. Later, you may have to appear before the DA and identify those men in his presence."

Before leaving, Richard reminded him, "The men you are working with are extremely dangerous desperados, for whom killing is a common affair. If they have the slightest doubt about your association with us, you know the consequence. So you should not contact them until you are ready with the software. Tell your friend also, not to contact them."

Richard reached his office and immediately called the expert computer software engineer, Bill, along with another engineer of Chinese origin, Michael Chang, who was engaged in investigating computer hacking cases for the CIA. He told them the problem and showed them the floppy of Chaoxiang, together with his instruction in Chinese.

"I give you two days for developing this software to a state where it can be demonstrated on a power system and work successfully. I will bring Chaoxiang to work with you. The user of this software should be convinced that it works," he told them and left the office.

Bill and Michael immediately sat down to study the floppy and make it appear usable. They also set up a miniature power station in the laboratory, to test the efficacy of the commands. Meanwhile, Richards left for Nevada to consult Aiguo on how to make this plan work. He had brought along a copy of Chaoxiang's floppy to seek his advice.

Aiguo ran the floppy on his computer and studied the program carefully, step by step. He then ran his own floppy which he used in the actual case and compared the two. After a study lasting more than two hours, he told Richard, "The program in Chaoxiang's floppy needs considerable additions, before it can be used in a real case. However, there is a short-cut to make it applicable in a very limited way. It can be used on a small network connected to a single power system. If you wait for another thirty minutes, I can write down the additional steps which are required and the codes necessary to operate it. I think it is sufficient to convince the thugs that this is a genuine software and applicable on a large scale."

After a wait of thirty minutes, Aiguo handed over a floppy to Richard, along with a set of instructions and codes. "You can test it on a small data network and let me know the result," he said. Richard flew back to Washington and arrived in his office with the new floppy. He called Bill and Michael to enquire about their progress. They said they have set up the miniature power system and were trying to modify the computer program to make it work.

He handed them the new floppy and said, "I got this from a professional hacker. You can fill in the codes and try it with the miniature system. If it works, I shall bring Chaoxiang and you can all sit together and make it work on a real system."

They experimented with the new floppy for a considerable time, without success. They were on the verge of giving up, when they succeeded in sending a command to the power system to shut down, bypassing the command loaded in its computer system. The power system was restarted again through another command. They informed Richard about their success.

Next day Richard went personally to the lodging place of Chaoxiang and brought him to the CIA headquarters. On the way he asked him if he had obeyed his directions and not communicated with anyone. He told him he did not tell anyone, but, Huang Fu was enquiring about the time he would take to complete the program. He had told him that he required at least one week. Richard told him to phone his brother informing him that he would be working with his friend to complete his project work, during the next three days.

He introduced Chaoxiang to Bill and Michael and told them to work together to test the floppy on a real power system. They identified the traffic signaling system in the eastern part of Philadelphia as the test site. They spent the next day gathering the necessary codes for the data network controlling the traffic signals. In the evening, the floppy was inserted in their computer and the command transmitted to the concerned data network. After a short interval all the traffic signals in the given area went off. It was restored after ten minutes. Richard was present and was very happy to witness it.

He told Chaoxiang, "You may now go back to your lodging and inform Huang Fu that the software is ready for a demonstration. You request him to take you to the Sugarhouse casino, Philadelphia, the next day for a live demonstration. Remember to wear your charm. It will protect you."

He ordered that Chaoxiang be dropped in his lodging and informed the FBI about his plan, requesting them to be ready for action.

Next day afternoon, Huang Fu drove to Philadelphia in his car, with Chaoxiang sitting next to him. They went straight to Sugarhouse casino. They were followed by secret services men, with their listening devices. At the entrance they were received by two men and taken to the cabin where George was waiting.

"So, is your software complete now? Are you ready to give a demonstration? Remember, we have no time to play games with you. If it works, you get your fifty grand, as promised. If it does not work, it will make me very angry and when I become angry, you can ask my men what happens!"

Chaoxiang replied, "We are ready to demonstrate. I'll run this floppy in your computer and within a few seconds, the traffic signals on the eastern part of the town will be shut off. After ten minutes I'll send another command and the signals will be switched on again. You can station your men in that part of the town to verify."

"I don't have to station my men there. I can see it on the TV screen in this room itself!" said George in a sarcastic tone.

Meanwhile, Richard went to Philadelphia to supervise things personally. He set up a few men in the computer centre network, which controls the traffic signals. Their job was to manually switch off the signals in case the floppy does not work. He contacted the FBI station Director to ensure that he has kept his armed men ready to raid the casino at a moment's notice. Satisfied that everything is set according to his plans, he remained in close contact with the secret services men who were monitoring their conversations.

It was planned that at the stroke of six, the floppy will be inserted in the computer and run. After a few seconds, all the signal lights in the eastern part of the city went off. Ten minutes later they were switched on again. The entire operation was visible on the TV screen in George's cabin. He was very happy and celebrated it with a drink.

"Let me try it out myself," he said after finishing his drink. He re-inserted the floppy disc and ran it. The result was the same. "I am impressed," he said. "Can the floppy ensure that all the lights in the city are switched off?"

"We have to insert certain codes for the data network that feeds the power system computer. These codes are classified and available with the department that manages the power system," said Chaoxiang.

"You work with us and we shall get you any data you want with our money and muscle power," bragged George. "I want all the lights in the city to be switched off."

Chaoxiang was hesitant to reply, "It may not be possible for me to work for you."

"Why not!" he thundered. "You'll get good money and perks, which includes wine and women."

Chaoxiang did not reply and kept grinning.

"Look! I am not accustomed to hearing 'no' for an answer. If I say you work with us, it means you work with us!" he said emphatically.

Huang Fu was persuading him to accept the offer, but he was thinking of an escape route.

Just then, there was a big commotion at the entrance door and a bevy of armed FBI men entered the casino, asking everyone to remain still with their hands over their heads. Some of them went straight into the cabin of George and pointed their guns at him saying, "You are under arrest for kidnapping, forceful confinement and waging war against the country."

George surrendered without showing any resistance. He was handcuffed by the FBI sleuths and taken outside the casino to a waiting armored van. Other men and women in the casino, including Chaoxiang and Huang Fu, were also handcuffed and taken to the FBI vans waiting outside. They were all driven to an unknown destination for interrogation.

Richard went back to his office and awaited news about the preliminary interrogations. Most of those arrested were released and George, together with his henchmen, a few bargirls and the duo of Huang Fu and Chaoxiang, were detained for further questioning. Della entered to inform him that Chaoxiang's brother has phoned her and desperately wants to meet her. Richard told her to call him to the CIA guesthouse in the afternoon. The detainees were transferred to the FBI headquarters for questioning. George refused to answer any question without the presence of his lawyer. His request for a lawyer was granted. Chauxiang and Huang Fu were kept in a separate room and since they both agreed to cooperate with the investigations, they were treated as the state's witness.

George's lawyer moved an application for bail on behalf of his client before the court, on the ground that he is a respectable citizen and owner of several businesses, which will suffer due to his detention. He also presented an argument that there was no evidence and he was wrongfully interned. The DA contested the application on the ground that the charges are very serious and the detainee being a person with enormous influence is likely to interfere in the investigations and intimidate witnesses. The court considered these views and denied bail to George, sending him to judicial custody for a period of ten days, pending completion of the investigation.

Chapter 19

Della reached the CIA guesthouse to await the arrival of Chaoxiang's brother. He arrived shortly, looking visibly disturbed.

"They arrested my brother on flimsy charges and have taken him for interrogation. He was not involved in any crime. He had just arrived from China and would have returned this week."

"Don't be upset! The only crime your brother has committed is that he agreed to help some dangerous criminals with his software, in exchange for money. I had warned him not to get involved with such people, as he is likely to be framed as their accessory. However, his greed for money overtook his sense of reasoning and that is why he found himself in this position."

"Now, how can I get him freed? You know he is not a criminal. He is a qualified engineer."

"Nothing can be done at this stage. Let the law take its course. You tell him to fully cooperate with the authorities. They might find him innocent and agree to deport him. I shall try to persuade them, through my contacts, that he is innocent."

He tried to look calm and said, "I shall give him your advice."He departed after thanking Della.

She returned to her office and reported everything to Richard. He was preparing to go to the FBI center to assist in the interrogation. He was taken to the room where George was being interrogated.

He asked George, "What is the extent of your business empire?"

"It's too big to describe in the time available. It is bigger than the empire of FBI !"

"Does it include power systems and traffic signals?"

George did not answer.

"I am repeating the question; does it include power systems and traffic signals? Please answer the question."

"No!" he said in loud, gruff voice.

"Do you know a Chinese software engineer by the name of Chaoxiang?"

"Never heard that name!"

"You were seen talking to him."

"I never talked with any Chinese engineer. We don't have any business in China."

"Do you know someone by the name of Max?"

"I know many persons by the name of 'Max.' In business circles this is a common name."

"This man is associated with a joint in Baltimore."

"Never heard of him!"

"If all the power systems in Philadelphia were to shut down by a faulty circuit, would it affect your business?"

"Yes, it would! Like all other businesses in the town."

"Do you have a computer in your office room?"

"Yes, I have!"

"Do you use it often? What sort of data is stored in its memory?"

"Yes, I use it whenever required. All data pertaining to my business is stored in it."

"Do you have a password and only you can operate it, or anyone can operate it."

"I have a password and mostly I operate it. Since some of the data is confidential, only my trusted aides are allowed to operate it."

Richard took out a floppy and asked, "George, do you remember having inserted this floppy and run it on your computer?"

"No! I never used this floppy. It seems unknown to me."

Richard inserted the floppy in a computer in the room and a sequence of prompts appeared on the screen. "Perhaps, now it will become easier for you to recognize it!" he said.

George stared at it for a couple of seconds, but gave no indication of recognizing it.

"Can you see these numbers? They are some codes for a particular network. Do you recognize it?" Richard asked.

George shook his head and feigned ignorance about these codes.

"I want to share some interesting facts with you. These codes pertain to the data network that is connected to the computer which controls the signal lights of the eastern part of the city. Our system engineers have been able to detect a command received by the system at 6 p.m. The command was traced to the IP address of the computer in your room. Apparently, that is the time that the command was sent from your computer. Can you tell us your location between 5.45 and 6.15 p.m.?" asked Richard.

George felt fidgety in his chair

"I was busy with my office work. Somebody must have sent it. I don't know."

"You don't know who sent it. A little while ago you said that only few trusted people are allowed to operate your computer. Who are your trusted people?"

"Anybody can operate it in my absence."

"You had said there is a password and nobody can operate it without your knowledge. It is clear that, either you yourself had sent the codes, or somebody else had sent it in your presence. Now tell us the facts."

George kept quiet and refused to answer the question.

Richard sent for Chaoxiang. When he came, he asked him, pointing towards George, "Do you recognize him?"

He nodded his head in the affirmative.

"Tell us in detail how you knew him and what were you doing between 5.45 p.m. and 6.15 p.m.?"

Chaoxiang began, "I was working in a project in my Center in Lanzhou, which deals with the development of a computer software to control the power supply to a city. It uses the data network which is connected to the computer system, to send commands for controlling the power supply. I was told by my friend, Huang Fu, that many people are interested in such projects here. So, I came all the way from China to sell my work to interested parties. Huang Fu contacted a friend named Max, who had many contacts in Philadelphia. He advised him to take me to the Sugarhouse casino and meet a person named George, who is sitting there. He told me to demonstrate the program before him and, if it is successful, he would pay me 50 grand."

"A few days later I met him again in the same place and demonstrated the program using his computer. The target power supply was the power to the traffic signals in the eastern part of the city. The codes that I used pertained to the data network of that particular power supply system. I t was successful and the traffic signals went off. The commands were sent at 6 p.m. I was in his room between 5.45 p.m. and 6.15 p.m. He was present in the room during that time and it was he, who inserted the floppy in the computer after opening it with a password."

"I don't know this man and he was never present in my room. I don't allow strangers to enter my room," he shouted.

Richard took out a recorder, which had recorded the conversation between him and Chaoxiang.

"Do you not believe your own voice as recorded in this instrument. This is the conversation between you and Chaoxiang, during the aforesaid time period?"

"This is not my voice. The recording is fake and manipulated," he insisted.

"George, the proceeding now, is being recorded and it is real, and not manipulated. We can entrust a qualified voice analyzer to test whether the voice recorded earlier and the voice recorded now, belong to the same person. Will that do?" he asked.

He was silent, but the arrogant expression on his face seen earlier, gave way to a feeling of abject surrender.

The FBI sleuths then took over and questioned him about his intention to forcibly make Chaoxiang work for him and not allowing him to leave the casino. He failed to give convincing replies. He was asked about the specific purpose of evincing interest in the software project. He eventually agreed that the purpose was to rob the banks and jewelry shops, after the power supply system in the city was shut down. Some of his henchmen were questioned about the activities in the casino. After being grilled for several hours they turned approvers and gave details of many illegal activities that were conducted in the casino, by the approval of George the names of certain prominent personalities figured in the orgies which were conducted.

Chapter 20

CIA Headquarters, Langley, Virginia

2 October 2013

John Epstein called a meeting in his special conference room and said, "This will be our last meeting to take stock of operation 'Dragon.' After the meeting, this file will be closed and the contents will remain a closely guarded secret for posterity, until it is declassified. The next generation may view the actions differently and draw their own conclusions."He asked Richard to give a review of the status of the operation.

Richard began, "The details about Flight TG-101 from Bangkok to London, are no longer discussed in the international media. In Bangkok, the plane in listed as "untraceable," since no signal could be picked up from the "black box" within thirty days, the period during which its battery remains active. In the first few days after the disappearance of the plane, there were strong protests from the Chinese Government on the inadequate search operations conducted by the Thai Government. They were concerned because they lost a number of qualified Chinese engineers. Now, they seem to be reconciled with the belief that the plane had crashed and there were no survivors. There were some investigations done individually by interested reporters and imaginative speculations put forward regarding the possible locations where it could have been hijacked. No conclusive evidence has been found to support these speculations. Operation 'Dragon' has still retained its lid on secrecy."

John asked," Did Diego Garcia figure in any speculation?"

"We had sent the international media on a wild goose chase by suggesting the involvement of certain Al Qaida outfits in the hijacking, with the objective of using the plane on some 9/11 type operation later. It seems to have been swallowed by them for some time and eventually died a natural death. One cranky reporter produced a photo believed to have been taken by someone on the island of Diego Garcia, but it had far too many holes to appear credible. Thereafter, the name of the island did not figure anywhere. Even the passengers in the plane did not know that they were in this island."

"We must compliment Harold for the meticulous way he had planned the whole operation. Clandestine operations can be a disaster for the organization planning it, if something goes wrong. I was very skeptical about its success when I first heard it. Now, I am glad we did it," he said.

"The credit goes to the men executing it, particularly our hero, Colonel Herman Turner along with partner Della. Only he could pilot the Boeing 777 with all its communication systems deactivated and land it on the narrow airstrip, in pitch darkness. It is a tragedy that his exploits can never be eulogized before the world, but remain confined to only the few of us," replied Harold.

"I know," he said. "I can never compliment him enough for what he has done for the nation knowing, that a slight mistake could have thrown his name into the dungeon of anonymity. Have they gone to Hawaii? I took it as my personal agenda to ensure that they get their well-deserved paid holiday. That is all I can do."

Richard looked across his shoulder to the right at the empty seat where Della usually sat when he is making a presentation. He felt proud that she played an important role in this achievement, but did not relish the idea of her sharing the glory with Herman. He continued with his presentation.

"The passengers of the plane were transported to Nevada, in a B-52 bomber aircraft which made only two service halts at US bases. No media reports have mentioned it, suggesting that nobody knew about it. The Boeing 777 aircraft was kept in the underground hangar and dismantled. The parts were packed in wooden boxes and transported in aC-5 transport plane to the south Indian Ocean and dumped into the sea. The existence of the plane has been obliterated forever."

"The Chinese and Russian software engineers are interned in Area 51, Nevada. They have agreed to their involvement in the development of illegal software, designed to disrupt our computer and data network and have also revealed the names of the organization supporting the project. They have agreed to work for us in projects given by us. They have signed undertakings to that effect. They are now fully cooperating with us, after showing initial hostility. On Wednesday June 26, there was a major power blackout in Moscow, which was done with the help of the Russian engineer, who used the program originally developed by them for use against our power supply system. This blackout was dubbed as the biggest energy emergency in Russia's history."

A faint smile appeared on the lips of John, as he commented, "It is like a boomerang which backfires on the initiator and injures him, instead of hitting the intended target. The matter is laudable because the Russian engineer, who was designing the program for use against us, has turned the barrel towards his own country! This is a lesson for politicians. If you try to hurt another country by developing a destructive weapon, it is possible the same weapon may hurt you, instead!"

Richard continued, "After the Russian adventure, another problem cropped up, which was not exactly a part of operation 'Dragon', but became linked to it. A Chinese software engineer who was working in the same center as our Chinese friend, Aiguo, came to USA with a similar software that was being developed by Aiguo and his Russian counterpart, Dr. Obukhov. It was by accident that we discovered the program in a floppy, abandoned on the bank of the Potomac. At first, it gave us the notion that the Chinese believed that Aiguo is alive and in our custody. He was, probably sent to try and trace him. Our investigation soon led us to him and we discovered that he was an ambitious Chinese engineer who wanted to make some money by selling his software. He had a Chinese friend living in Baltimore, who had contacts with the underworld and was helping him find a buyer for his product."

"Initially, this Chinese lad, named Chaoxiangi, was adamant and refused to divulge anything. At this stage, I must admit that Della's knowledge of Chinese was a great help. She could persuade him to wear a 'charm' that was meant to be sent to her friend in China. Actually, this 'charm' was a miniature transmitter to transmit the conversations to a recorder carried by a secret service man nearby. It facilitated tracking him and knowing his plans. We used our 'plan 2' to get him involved with drugs and got him arrested. We got him released on bail and started interrogating him.

Using Aiguo's help we learnt that the computer program he was possessing was incomplete and needed more additions to make it applicable for the purpose he was seeking. We volunteered to help him complete the program, if he agreed to help us nab the underworld men."

"We came to know that the mafia don, George Borgasi, agreed to pay him an advance of fifty grand if he demonstrated his software's ability to switch off power supply systems. We gathered that the purpose was to rob banks and jewelry shops in Philadelphia after switching off the computer controlled power supply system. We helped Chaoxiang complete the software and demonstrate it on the traffic signal in the eastern part of Philadelphia. On the appointed day, he ran the software from George's computer in his cabin and switched off the power supply to the signal lights. He was impressed and was forcing Chaoxiang to work for him in developing software for switching off the power supply in the whole town. This was the time when the FBI sleuths entered the casino of George and arrested him on charges of kidnapping, forcible confinement and attempting to wage war against the nation.'

"We thus came to know a sinister plot by the mafia don to disrupt the essential services in the city. Our investigations led to many illegal activities that were carried out in the casino under the guise of entertainment business. The sordid details emerged when a few henchmen in the service of George, decided to become approvers and spilled the beans. The casino was used as a venue for orgies, in which many eminent people participated. Some of the prominent names that were revealed would shock everyone. We also learnt that the Internal Revenue Department is also taking active interest in this case, because many cases of fraud and cheating were reported in the past, but no evidences were found to book them."

"It would appear that the entry of the Chinese engineer to USA was a 'red herring', but it now seems it was related to the initial joint venture between the Chinese secret service and the KGB, to disrupt all essential services in USA and totally paralyze the economy. This lead was taken up by the young lad to make a quick buck. This was also, perhaps, his way of seeking revenge at being removed from the main project and the retention of Aiguo. It was an act of Providence that the bag containing the floppy was discovered, which led to the unraveling of the criminal activities," commented John.

"All's well that ends well!" said Richard. "The culprits in this case have been charged and are due to face trial. The magnitude of the evidence that have been collected will make it very tough for them to find an escape route. Through this case, we have also unearthed the names of the other gangsters who were linked to them. One very good thing that has happened is that the Chinese and Russian software engineers, who had earlier teamed together to work against us, have now joined us and are engaged in the development of new tools to prevent future Cybercrimes. They appear to be happy working here and are not expressing any desire to go back to their respective motherlands. Since they don't exist officially, being presumed to be dead in the plane crash, they have no fear of having to face punitive actions by their respective secret services."

John was happy at the way this top secret operation was carried out. He delivered his last speech as head of the CIA, as he was due to retire from service at the end of the month.

"In my thirty-five years of service to protect the interests of this country, most of them as an under- cover agent, sleuth and eventually an intelligence officer, I have indulged in all kinds of activities, subversive, political, patriotic and many others. I have given my best in whatever capacity I was used and taken up any responsibility that was assigned to me. I have no regrets. Of course, I was lucky to be aided by a team of very competent comrades, whose company I shall never forget. It is now time to look over to the other side of the hill at the life that awaits me."

"Before I look over the hill, it is appropriate to look back and see what I have done. I started my career at a time when the cold war between the two major powers was at its highest point. I remember the time when I was posted in Moscow, it was discovered that the bricks in our embassy building conference rooms had small chips embedded in them to eavesdrop all conversations that took place in that room. After that, a decision was taken to have full glass cubicles suspended between the floor and the ceiling, in which the discussions were held. This was retaliated by our Government and bugs were surreptitiously planted in the Russian embassy in Washington to eavesdrop all conversations. Today, when I think of it, it appears as childishness and not the act of mature men."

"Another famous incident was the arming of the smaller countries surrounding the two powers, with nuclear weapons. The Americans created NATO to arm the countries surrounding Russia with the latest military hardware and nuclear arsenal. The Russians retaliated with the arming of Cuba with nuclear weapons. At the nick of time, in a sudden display of statesmanship, both the powers agreed to suspend the process and reverse whatever was already done. This 'eye for eye, tooth for tooth policy' almost brought the two super powers on the brink of war. Hasn't somebody said that this policy would eventually lead to all the people in either country, blind and toothless? There can be no victor in such a war,"

"We have come a long way from those times, but the trend still seems to persist. When Russia decided to increase its sphere of influence by invading Afghanistan under a flimsy pretext, the Americans decided to create a monster under the name of Osama-bin Laden, an anti-communist crusader and an heir to royal family in Saudi Arabia. He was given money and the responsibility to recruit and train Mujhadeens to fight the Russian forces. Sophisticated arms training facilities were provided in USA by my organization. Gradually, Americans stepped into the Gulf area, ostensibly to settle the dispute between Iraq, Kuwait and Saudi Arabia regarding stealing of crude oil from each other's oil wells."

"Our entry into the 'sacred' Muslim soil of the Gulf, infuriated Osama and he turned his wrath on us. He was disowned by the Saudi Arabia rulers, at our insistence, and driven away from his country. He took refuge in Afghanistan and the men he recruited and trained to fight against the Russians, were told to aim their guns at us, too. From a position of friend, he became one of our bitterest enemies. He organized one of the largest army of religious fanatics, under a group named Al Qaida. They started their destructive activities on American lives and properties, culminating in the famous 9/11 incident. We know the amount of damage to innocent lives caused by this senseless action. People who had nothing to do with the super power politics lost their lives. He derived sadistic pleasure in the fact that he had destroyed the commercial hub of America, located in the twin towers and brought them to their knees. Human lives had no value to him. Who had created this Frankenstein monster? Unfortunately, we have to take the blame."

"Sometimes we do things with the purpose of hurting someone, but, like a boomerang, it comes back to hurt us. Even now, a very similar thing happened when the Russians and Chinese wanted to hurt us. But, this time they got hurt and we luckily escaped. People change, governments change, but the fallacies still remain. We never learn by our mistakes. Starting from Vietnam, in the early sixties, we are still prone to interfering in the affairs of other countries and get bogged down into a helpless state from where it is difficult to come out."

"You may ask, why am I saying all these unpatriotic things now? Wisdom comes with age, but not while you are in the Government. I am now on the verge of retirement and my wisdom is working. Perhaps, you will also do the same, when you are in my present position. We first create a puppet and then pamper him with all the toys, like money, guns and bombs. He grows into a powerful monster killing our enemies and faithfully following our commands. We feel proud of him, until one day he feels he no longer needs our commands and takes decisions on his own. Then we condemn him and finally kill him. This is what we did with Osama bin laden and many others before him, like Saddam Husain, Manuel Noriega, etc. We shall continue to pursue this policy, irrespective of whosoever comes to power."

At this point Richard intervened with the news that George has confessed all his crimes and agreed to disclose the names of his partners and all his illegal business.

John was overjoyed and said, "See! It is like digging for the earthworm and discovering a poisonous snake! You should ensure that he spends his whole life in prison, because if he comes out he will again start his old business by force of habit."

Richard disclosed another news, "The Chinese and Russian Engineers have begun work on a new project to develop software for preventing future Cybercrimes. They will ensure that our networks are completely free from Cyber-attacks, with a built-in capability to identify the source of the incoming rogue signals."

"That is superb! But, you never know, somebody may develop another technique to overcome these security measures!" He said. "This idea of motivating criminals to use their brains in constructive work benefitting the country, instead of in crime, is brilliant. Criminals usually have very intelligent minds, which help them to keep ahead of the law enforcing agencies and evade arrest. If they can be harnessed to help nab other criminals they can be very efficient in their job. I have seen the biopic on the famous fraudster, Frank Abagnale, who used to forge checks so intelligently that the FBI could never catch him. Eventually, he was caught by a very intelligent agent, who persuaded him to work for the FBI in detecting other check frauds. In later life, he saved the country billions of dollars, by not only detecting fraudulent checks, but also designing checks which cannot be forged easily. I foresee a repeat of this story."

Harold raised a pertinent question, "Is it necessary to indulge in clandestine actions to achieve our objectives? If we are against the law breakers, we should not ourselves break the law."

John smiled as he answered, "I can see what you are hinting at! The playing arena is not always uniform. The criminals fire the first shot and we have to follow the direction of the shot and return the fire. They lead and we follow. There are two ways of overtaking them. First, we take a shortcut and arrive at the anticipated destination, before them, if the destination is known precisely. Secondly, we prevent them from reaching the destination. Usually, the second option is used, for which we have to often resort to clandestine methods. Although it may appear to be illegal, its purpose is to prevent a much greater illegal activity, which can cause immense damage to the country. Seen in this context, I do not think that clandestine activities can be really termed illegal, provided it is done in a legal way."

Harold wondered how one can term "kidnapping," as legal.

John answered, "If a murderer has planned to kill a dozen people and you kidnap him, then you have prevented him from carrying out his plan. In effect, you have saved dozen lives. Is it illegal? In your action in operation 'Dragon', you have kidnapped more than two hundred passengers. If all the passengers had reached their destination, the destructive software would have been used on our power supply system, shutting out power in the northern region of USA. You know how much damage it could have caused in terms of life and property? See the power blackout in Russia! How many people have lost their lives in metros, road accidents, hospitals and jumping from the building in sheer panic? If so much damage has occurred in one town, you can imagine how much damage would have been caused by a blackout in many cities! Thus, kidnapping a plane load of passengers has saved the lives of thousands of people, apart from destruction of properties."

Richard announced that a small party has been arranged to mark the completion of operation "Dragon" and bid farewell to John, by a select group of staff members who were directly associated with this operation. He invited them to the lecture hall for an open question and answer session over snacks and drinks.

***

John was received at the entrance of the hall by his deputy and taken to the dais where he was presented a bouquet. He read out a brief record of John's association with the organization. He requested him to say a few words and participate in the question and answer session.

A young officer who had joined recently asked the first question, "While taking a tour of the CIA headquarters, I saw James Sanborn's sculptures at the entrance, known as the Kryptos. There are enigmatic messages displayed in four different codes. Only three of these codes have been solved and the fourth remains unsolved. If solving complex codes is one of the functions of CIA, how is it that the code at the entrance to the headquarters remains unsolved?

"Excellent question?" remarked John. "You certainly possess keen observation power and also intelligence and I'm sure you will make an excellent intelligence officer. I'm not saying this to avoid answering your question. I shall certainly answer it. When George Carlin saw a half full glass of water he had only two choices: whether to call it half full or half empty. He later added a third choice; glass is twice as big as the volume of water. When a CIA agent sets down to crack a complex code, there are a large number of diverse choices from which to choose the right interpretation. The code writer always tries to make the connections as complex as possible, e. g., a particular alphabet is connected to a certain number, which is connected to a particular day of the month, and so on. Deciphering the right connections requires tremendous patience, diligence and intelligence. It is a battle between the code writer and the decipherer. If the decipherer wins, the code is cracked, otherwise the code remains unsolved. Although CIA has some of the most intelligent people, in this case, apparently, the code writer has won. You may be the one who will challenge the code writer and win."

Another officer asked, "If you are given a choice to choose a particular career in your next birth, will it be CIA?"

John laughed and said, "I don't know if I will be reborn as a man, or an animal! If I'm born as a man, I shall certainly choose a career in the CIA once again. There is no other service where a person has the opportunity to take up tough challenges in both covert and overt actions. Success increases your confidence, while failures diminish it. One has to be mentally tough to withstand failures and convert it into success."

The celebration ended with a get-together over drinks and snacks.